Better Late Than Never

Stephanie Morris

Amira Press, LLC

Better Late Than Never
Stephanie Morris

All rights reserved.
Copyright © June 2009 Stephanie Morris
Cover Art Copyright © June 2009 Amira Press

This is a work of fiction. All characters and events portrayed in this novel are fictitious or used fictitiously. All rights reserved, including the right to reproduce this book, or portions thereof, in any form.

ISBN: 978-1-935348-40-5

Publisher:
Amira Press, LLC
Baltimore, MD
www.amirapress.com

Dedication

To my mom who always told me to never give up on my dreams, and to my brother who has always taught me to dream big.

Chapter One

Randy smiled to himself when he looked over at his three-year-old son, Wade. He was taking him to enroll him into the new day care center that had just been opened. Being the sheriff of Appling County was a tough and demanding job at times, but he loved it. The downside was that there were times when he was on call twenty-four-seven, but when he wasn't, he spent all of his time with Wade. His son was his life. One of his deputies, Gary, had recommended the new day care. His sister had enrolled her children and had nothing but good things to say about the day care and its owner. She seemed to work very well with children. There were two other day care centers in Baxley, but Gary was a pretty reliable guy, so Randy was going to take his advice and look at the day care center. His mother had been watching Wade when he needed her to, but she was getting up in age, and she shouldn't have to keep a rambunctious three-year-old, whether she enjoyed it.

He cut off the engine to his truck after he pulled up in front of the decorative building. It would appeal to the eye of a child. Hoisting his thirty-two-year-old body out, he walked around to the passenger side and opened the door to the back seat. Wade had been an excuse for him to get the larger truck he always wanted. Randy's frame was too large for a car. It was dangerous for a child Wade's age to ride in the front seat, even if he was in a car seat. So the double cab truck was the perfect solution. He unbuckled Wade out of his car seat, Wade hopped into his arms, and Randy shut the door to the truck. He made his way up the steps. Randy opened the door and stepped inside. It closed behind him but not loud enough to draw the attention of the woman who stood behind the counter. He grinned when he recognized her.

They had grown up together in Baxley, although she was four years younger than him. In high school, he and her older brother Max had been good friends and had played on the football team together.

"Morning, Zeb."

She looked up in surprise then smiled.

"Good morning, Sheriff. Good morning, Wade. What brings the two of you to this side of town?"

"I came to see if I could enroll Wade into day care here."

Zebbie gave him a concerned look. "Is your mom sick?"

He shook his head. "No, but the fact you just asked the question let's me know I'm doing the right thing."

Zebbie reached under the counter and pulled out a clipboard with paperwork on it. "Fill this out, and when you are finished, let me know."

He nodded and walked over to the chair and took a seat. If he didn't know any better he would say Zebbie looked nervous, although he couldn't figure out why. Shrugging the thought off he turned his attention to the paperwork in front of him. Wade settled onto his lap, and he began to fill out the paperwork. They were simple questions like Wade's age, if he was potty trained, and other questions to determine how much individual attention Wade needed. Once Randy answered all of the questions, he handed the clipboard to Zebbie. She gave the paperwork a once-over, then looked up at him.

"Okay, follow me to the conference room."

They were led to a room with a large table and three chairs. There was also a small table with four little chairs and a large toy box sitting next to it. Wade eyed them with obvious hope and then looked up at him. Zebbie left the room, and Randy led Wade to the table where they could have a seat.

"You will have to wait to see if you can play with the toys."

Wade nodded like he had all of the patience in the world, a deception that would fool any person who hadn't been in the presence of his son for more than five minutes. While Wade was well behaved, it would dissipate. Wade ventured over to the smaller table and sat in one of the chairs. It resembled the set he had at home. Randy glanced down at his watch just when the door opened. He froze in surprise when he saw who stood there. It was Kristen, the only woman he ever loved and had never been able to tell.

* * * *

Shocked, Kristen stared at the man in front of her. She fought the instant reaction of wanting to rub her eyes to make sure they weren't deceiving her. It had been six years since she had last seen him. Six years that she tried to forget him, and now, she realized it had all been in vain. She was more in love with him now than she had been when she was a teenager. He seemed to have become more handsome than she recalled. His brown eyes still held the mystery they used to, and his light blond hair was cut short, yet still long enough to show his hand had been raked through it several times despite the early hour. He looked taller. His shoulders were broader, and he it looked as though he exercised to stay in shape judging by the way his uniform fit.

Kristen gave herself a mental shake. What was she doing? Drooling over a man whom she shouldn't be. Looking down at the paperwork in her hands, she used the distraction to collect her thoughts and herself. If she had read it before entering the room, she wouldn't have been unprepared. It was too late to think about that now. She stepped farther into the room and closed the door behind her. Walking over to Randy, she held her hand out to him and hoped he would shake it.

"It is a pleasure to see you again, Mr. Stroud."

Before he could react to her formal attitude, Kristen continued. "Wade is more than welcome to enroll at the day care center. I would like to explain some things to you about the operations of my center, and then you make your final decision."

Her gaze drifted over to Wade, and another pang traveled through her chest. He was a carbon copy of Randy, and he should be their son but wasn't. What made it even worse was that there was no reason why he wasn't.

Randy had walked away from her with no explanation at all. After walking over to the little boy, she knelt beside him.

"Hi, Wade. My name is Ms. Smith."

He gave her a brief look then looked to his father for approval. When Randy gave it, Wade smiled before speaking. "Hi, Ms. Smith."

"How old are you, Wade?"

"Three."

Kristen's mouth curled upward in amusement. He was such a sweetheart. "Do you see the box over there?"

He nodded eagerly, and she grinned. She explained to him that it was full of toys he could play with while she talked to his dad. "But you must put the toys up when you are finished playing with them."

He agreed to the bargain, and she stood. Once she was out of his way, he headed to the toy box. She walked over to where Randy was sitting and took the empty chair next to him.

"You are good with kids."

"Thank you. Now to discuss the business of . . ." She stopped when Randy's hand touched hers.

"How have you been?"

"Fine, now if we could get—"

"Talk to me, Kristen."

She shook her head and tried to pull her hand back, but he wouldn't let her. "There is nothing to talk about, Mr. Stroud."

He refused to let her distract him with her formality. Instead, he leaned forward. "Yes, there is."

"What is there to talk about?"

"You can tell me how you have been."

"I already have."

"Kristen, I know we didn't end on a good note, but the past is the past."

Her eyebrows rose in disbelief. "It may be easy for you, but it isn't easy for me. You know me well enough to know that I don't make the same mistake twice."

"Kristen, we—"

She held up her hand. "A long time ago, you broke my heart, and it took a long time for the wound to heal. Needless to say, I don't want to open the wound again." She looked down at the papers she was organizing. Her hand trembled before she steadied it. "Now, if you want, Wade can stay today. I will just need you to fill out these forms and he can."

As she handed the forms to him, she explained what they were. One was a medical emergency form giving them permission to take Wade to the hospital if needed. Another asked about his history of health and immunizations. The last form explained the payment that was expected and when.

"Do you have any questions?"

He shook his head, and she knew he was being dishonest. His eyes told her he was.

"Not at the moment."

Kristen knew he had as many questions for her as she had for him, and none of her questions was related to the paperwork.

"Good, then fill out these forms and he can stay today."

He remained silent, but she could feel his gaze burning a hole into her, and she looked up. "Is something wrong?"

He shook his head. "I was just looking at how beautiful you are?"

She wanted to disagree with him, but his heated stare told her he still believed it. Her curly dark brown hair fell a few inches below her shoulder blades. Randy had always loved her hair and in the past could never resist touching it. Today, she had pulled her hair back into a French braid, a style that complemented her creamy cocoa colored face. She stared at him with milk chocolate eyes she tried to keep devoid of emotion, and it was a difficult task. Letting Randy go after he broke up with her had been hard to do, and now with all of the emotions bubbling to the surface at the sight of him, Kristen wondered if she had ever really moved on.

Looking down at his left hand, she looked for a ring or a ring tan line, and when she didn't find one, she frowned. From what she heard, he should be married. Was he divorced? She tampered down the excitement rising to the surface. Baxley wasn't a small place, but with a population a little under forty-five hundred, a few major events still got around. Like it had when she and her sisters had moved to Baxley with their mother. To this day, they were the only triplets to have lived in Baxley.

She was pulled from her thoughts when he leaned forward and brushed his hand against her cheek. Her eyes widened with weariness, and she had to force herself not to pull away. She couldn't let him know his touch affected her.

"Give me a chance, Kristen."

She did pull away then. This was exactly what she didn't want. Couldn't afford to give into. She already suffered one heartache, and that was plenty.

"Give you a chance to what?"

He gave her a gentle smile. "I want a chance to make things right between us."

Kristen shook her head. It was something she couldn't allow to happen. She looked over at Wade. "I don't think your wife would approve." Randy held up his left hand. She furrowed her eyebrows together in puzzlement. She heard he had married six years ago, but she hadn't heard anything about a divorce. "Are you one of those guys who doesn't wear a wedding ring?"

His lips curled upward. "I'm not married, and I never have been."

She remained silent. That only meant she didn't know Randy like she thought she did. He always seemed to be the kind of guy that would do the honorable thing and marry the mother of his child.

"Then his mother wouldn't approve of it."

He shrugged. "I doubt she would even be concerned."

The comment bothered her. How could he be so unconcerned about flirting with one woman while he was involved with another? Randy continued speaking, not giving her the chance to respond.

"I know I hurt you. I also know I made a mistake. It is a mistake I plan to correct. I wanted you six years ago, and I want you now although this time it is for keeps."

Kristen pulled away and stood up. "Finish filling out these papers, and I will take Wade and show him the rest of the center."

At the mentioning of his name, Wade looked up. Kristen walked over to him. "Would you like to take a look around?"

He looked over at his father, and when Randy nodded. Wade did the same. That Wade always wanted approval from his father before he made contact with strangers was comforting. She held out her hand, and he took it. "We are going to meet some of the children your age."

She led him from the conference room to the main room. This was the room where the three-, four-, and five-year-olds spent the majority of their time.

"This is where you will spend a lot of time." She explained this would be the place where he would improve his counting and alphabet, writing, and drawing skills. "This is also the place where you will take your nap."

Wade frowned at the idea, which gave her the indication that naptime wasn't his favorite activity, and she laughed as she led him out of the room. She showed him the kitchen where he would eat breakfast, lunch, and a snack. Wade's face lit up at the mention of food.

"Now it is time to meet some of your classmates."

She led him to a large room where all of the kids were sitting, waiting for story time. "This is where we come for story time. Would you like to stay and hear the story?"

"Yes."

She led him over to his age group. "Good morning, everyone. This is Wade, and he is going to be joining us today."

Everyone welcomed him, and his face lit up. She knelt down in front of him. "I need to finish speaking with your dad, but I will be back to check on you."

He nodded, and she stood and took a deep breath trying to prepare herself to go back in to talk to Randy. When she returned to the conference room, he looked up briefly. She studied him when he looked down to add his signature to the last page. She blinked when he shuffled the papers back into their original order and handed them back to her.

"Would you like for Wade to stay today?"

"Yes. I will be back to pick him up at six."

"That is fine. Our hours are five in the morning to six-thirty in the evening. If there is ever a time when you are running late, just call and let us know."

He stood. "If I am running late, my mom or dad will come and pick him up. I put them down as the next of kin. They also have permission to pick him up when I can't do so."

Kristen smiled. "Okay."

A strange expression materialized on his face, and she wondered what he was thinking. Curiosity coursed through her, and she fought it. She wanted to know, but she wasn't going to ask. The last thing she should do was give him any indication there was any interest on her part. Instead she walked him to the entrance of her day care.

"It was good to see you again," she replied casually.

He grinned. "It was good to see you, too."

She wanted to stand there and watch as Randy got into his truck and drove off but knew it would be a bad idea. Instead, she turned and headed back into the day care. For the first time since Randy walked into, she allowed herself to react. Her knees gave out, and she collapsed against the wall. Randy had a way of making her weak in the knees. It was more than his sexiness. Randy always affected her in a way that no other man had. To be honest, she was surprised she was just now running into him. Kristen would never admit that she had been trying to avoid him. She had done a good job up until now. The only thing she wondered was if he was using Wade to get to her. She wasn't the only person with a day care center. He had to have known this day care center was hers. Then again, she hadn't placed any official advertisements. It hadn't been needed. Word of mouth traveled faster.

Still, to have him show up with his son had hurt. When she found out about Wade several years ago, she had been upset. It bothered her that the son Randy had wasn't with her. Wade should have been theirs. He would have been if Randy hadn't called off their relationship. What had annoyed her even more was the fact that he had moved on. She hadn't moved. She never had. There was no one else for her. She knew from the time she laid eyes on him. Randy was a good man. He had always been good to her. Even today she was puzzled as to why Randy had called their relationship to an end.

What irritated her now was he thought he could just walk back into her life and they could pick up where they left off. She didn't like it, and she wouldn't fall for it. After the way Randy broke her heart, he would have to prove that he wanted her back. Shaking her head to clear it, she groaned. She was going to hear it from her sisters when she made it home this evening, but it would be worth it because she needed their advice on this one.

* * * *

The rest of the day went by quickly without any extra events, and she was thankful. She locked up the building and said good-bye to Zebbie and Gerri before getting into her car and driving the short distance to the house she shared with her sisters. In some ways it was strange to be back in the house she and her sister's grew up in when they returned to Baxley. On the other hand it was good to be back in the place she always considered to be home.

It was interesting being a triplet, and it was fun. Kristen had been born with two best friends, and they knew everything about each other. They had always lived together. She and her sisters had the privilege of having wonderful parents who had died way too soon if you asked her. Their father had been a police officer when they were little and they had lived in Atlanta, Georgia. One night, while on assignment, he had been killed in the line of duty. They had been ten years old at the time, and it had been devastating, so devastating that they had moved in with their mother's grandparents in Baxley. It had been a good move for their mother to make even though she died of an aneurysm right after they graduated from high school.

To her, it had always seemed like their mother had hung on long enough to make sure she and her sisters would be okay after she was gone. She and her sisters had been okay. They had left Baxley for Athens to attend the University of Georgia. Their maternal grandmother had passed away right after they had graduated from college with their undergraduate degree, and their maternal grandfather had passed away two years ago. They talked to their father's parents at least once a month, but it was rare that they saw them since they were busy traveling the country in an RV. Kristen sighed when she pulled up in front of her grandparents' house. Overall, life had been good.

Just a month ago, they had finalized their move back to Baxley because they decided they wanted to live their lives out in Baxley. They wanted to settle down, get their careers off the ground, and, hopefully, marriage and children would follow. They all had a lot of pleasant memories of the town. She got out of her car and started up the walkway. Kayla, her oldest sister, opened the door before she could even get to the porch.

"What is wrong?"

She laughed. The other thing about having identical sisters was that they knew something was wrong with each other prior to anything being said. Kayla pulled her inside.

"Well whatever it is, we will talk about it over dinner. Go freshen up." She closed the door and moved off in the other direction before Kristen could get a word out.

Shaking her head, Kristen headed upstairs and dropped her purse and her bag on the bed. She walked into the bathroom and washed her hands and her face then went back downstairs. Keirra was setting the table.

Kayla was the oldest by three minutes. Keirra came next in birth order, leaving her to be the youngest of the trio.

"Need any help?"

Keirra kissed her on the cheek. "No, but you look like you have had a hard day. Have a seat and rest."

She sat down and sighed. A short while later, the table was set and Kayla was dishing out spaghetti and cornbread. They ate in silence until suddenly Keirra asked the question that would set them up for the discussion of the night. A discussion she was dreading.

"So what happened today?"

"Randy enrolled his three-year-old son into my day care."

Kayla began to choke on the cornbread she had just taken a bite of, and Keirra patted her on the back and frowned. "The cop?"

Kristen shook her head. Sometimes, Keirra could be so obtuse. "He is a county sheriff, and don't start."

Keirra was a very law-abiding citizen, but she did have an aversion to cops.

Kayla ignored Keirra. "Forget the cop part. I'm more concerned about him being the man that broke your heart. What did you do?"

She shrugged. "I handled it like any professional would."

"Did you at least cuss at him?"

Keirra chuckled. "Kristen doesn't know how."

Actually, she did know how. She just never did because she was too reserved and sometimes too shy to do so. She was the peacemaker of the three sisters. Kayla was the rational of the three, and Keirra was the straightforward one. Somehow the straight forwardness had always managed to get them into trouble.

"No, I didn't. There was no need to."

"Is he still married?"

She paused trying to figure out how to inform her sisters of the interesting information she had learned today. Knowing her sisters like she did, she knew the best way to tell them something was to tell them something straight out.

"It seems it was just a rumor. He was never married."

Keirra rolled her eyes. "Well that puts things into a different perspective, doesn't it?"

She nodded slowly, realizing just how true her sister's words were. "Yes, it does."

Chapter Two

"It isn't nice to hit people, Susan."

The little girl looked up at her with woeful eyes, and Kristen turned her attention to Michael.

"And it isn't nice for you to push people because you feel they are in your way. Do each of you understand why what you did was wrong?"

Both children nodded, and she stood. "You two will have to spend some time in the Quiet Corner to think about what you did."

Both children's faces fell, but neither said a word because they knew they were in trouble. She would probably be in trouble herself because now she would have to explain to two sets of parents why one child was going to have a nice black eye and why the other had skinned knees and ripped pants. She sat Susan in one corner and Michael in the other, leaving them in Zebbie's care then returned outside. Gerri was having a hard time keeping all of the kids in line and seemed happy to see her. Kristen took over the three-year-olds trying to keep them from hurting each other. A few moments later, Gerri came to stand over by her.

"So I hear you have a date with Randy tonight?"

She gave Gerri a dry look before rolling her eyes. "I guess there are some things that haven't changed about Baxley."

Gerri grinned, and Kristen smiled in return. "Who told you?"

"Mom ran into Mrs. Stroud at the store, and she mentioned it."

Kristen groaned. "Technically, it isn't a date. I am just having dinner at his parents'."

Gerri's eyebrows rose. "You have to excuse me because I have been out of the dating game for a while, but normally going over to have dinner with a guy's parents isn't insignificant."

Kristen shook her head at Gerri. "Yes, but everyone knows Randy and I have history. I have always been close to his parents and have spoken to them off and on over the years."

"Hot and heavy history," Gerri added.

"And you are melodramatic."

Gerri smirked. "I guess that is the reason why I got all of the starting roles in the school plays."

Kristen laughed. "Gerri, you are a walking play."

Gerri looked at her with a look of shock that Kristen found humorous. "If your acting ability didn't come in handy with the kids, I might let your statement knock my confidence down a little."

Kristen shook her head again at her friend and co-worker's antics. They had known each other for a long time, and when she told Gerri she and her sisters were coming back to Baxley, there had been nothing but excitement. Gerri had also been excited when she asked her to work at the day care. Kristen had worked with Gerri on getting the right certifications, and everything else had gone well.

"Gerri, it would take a two-thousand-pound brick to knock your confidence loose an inch."

Before Gerri could respond, Kristen put her whistle in her mouth and blew. The kids stopped playing and began to line up. Once everyone had been accounted for, they headed into the building and straight to their tables for snack time.

"What are we having today?" Gerri asked.

Kristen shrugged. "Something the kids will enjoy."

The snack consisted of half a chicken salad sandwich with cutup raw vegetables and fruit.

"So how serious is this date between you and Randy?"

Kristen sighed heavily, knowing the subject wasn't going to be dropped until Gerri received the answer she wanted.

"Well, first off, this isn't a date. It is Randy's way of sucking up to me to try to get me to go out with him on a date."

Gerri almost choked on her sandwich, and Kristen laughed. Gerri shook her head. "You can be so sneaky sometimes."

Kristen just shrugged and ate a carrot. She and her sisters had gotten away with their share of devious activities.

"So are you interested in him?"

Kristen answered honestly. "I don't think there was ever a time when I wasn't interested in him." She finished off her vegetables. "To be honest, I can't say no to him. I never could. However, I do plan on taking things a lot slower this time. There are a few things that Randy and I have to work out."

Gerri nodded while she finished off her sandwich. "Yes, you should make him *work* for it. He needs to know that he was a fool to walk away from you."

Kristen's mouth gapped open as she watched her friend get up and walk off. Only Gerri could say such a response with a straight face and make it sound so dirty. Even so she did plan on making Randy work to earn her back.

* * * *

Kristen sat behind the wheel of her midsize SUV doubting herself. She gave into the weakness briefly before she climbed out of her car. Somehow, Randy had managed to coerce her into coming over to his parents' house for dinner. It had been a while since she had seen the Strouds. She missed them. The last time she had seen them, it had been at her grandmother's funeral. But she soon found out not much had changed in the Strouds household. The evening flew by, and soon she and Randy were sitting on the front porch in the swing enjoying the breeze. Dinner had been wonderful, and she was stuffed. She glanced over at Randy when he reached out and touched the thick braid that hung over her shoulders.

"Do you ever wear your hair down?"

She shook her head. "Not in a long time. Six years to be exact."

"Why not?"

"You know it is hard to manage when I wear it down."

He smiled, his expression telling her he remembered it very well from when they dated. "Then why don't you cut it?"

She rolled her eyes in frustration. "I like it long and because Kayla and Keirra would kill me. Our hair is one of the traits we inherited from our father."

He shook his head, but his smile stayed in place. The statement made perfect sense to anyone who knew Kristen and her sisters.

"Will you let it down for me?"

She started to say no, but instead, she reached up and pulled the band from around the end of her ponytail. With a few flicks of her wrist, she had her ponytail down. Her hair fell over her shoulders. He reached over and ran his fingers through her hair. She shivered and leaned into his touch until she realized what she was doing and pulled away.

"You are so beautiful."

She could feel herself begin to flush, and he grinned. Somehow he had always managed to make her feel like she was the most beautiful woman in the world. Still she couldn't let that weaken her resolve. Randy owed her an explanation before she could allow herself to accept his embrace.

"I always thought you were even more beautiful when you blushed."

Blushing harder, she shook her head and looked away. Sometimes she hated her medium brown skin tone. A blush could show up, and when it did, it was clear indication she was embarrassed. He laughed, and she gasped when he pulled her onto his lap.

"Randy, what are you doing?"

He tilted her chin upward. "Getting ready to kiss you."

Kristen saw his mouth coming toward hers, yet she couldn't stop him, couldn't resist. She knew she should, but she wanted to feel his lips on hers one more time. Her response was slow and shy, but Randy's was the exact opposite. He took her mouth in a demanding kiss. One that took everything she had to give.

This kiss was different than the ones they had shared in the past. There was no hesitance in his kiss. Gone was the boy she had fallen in love with, and in his place was a man. A man she wasn't certain she knew, and with the way he was kissing her, she wasn't certain it mattered. She gasped when he slid his tongue between her lips and into her mouth. His kiss spoke of experience in pleasuring a woman. She knew most of it had come from her, but she could never remember their kisses being this steamy. Moaning, she leaned closer to him and allowed his tongue to delve deeper into her mouth. Pulling back, she gasped for air and trembled when he began placing kisses along her throat. She moaned before his lips found their way back to hers. Her arms crept up around his neck, and his arms tightened around her waist.

She broke the kiss off and buried her face against his shoulder when his hands found her breasts. His hand slid under her shirt, and she stiffened. What in the hell was she doing? She wasn't sending the right signal at this moment. Lifting her hand, she caught his wrist and held it. After he didn't get the hint, she tried to remove his hands.

"Randy, we have to stop."

Her words didn't seem to register, and she started to struggle against him. They were moving too fast. She had to slow down. They had to slow down.

"*Randy!*"

He broke off his sensual assault on her throat, a look of concern on his face.

"What is wrong?"

Kristen removed his hands and slid out of his lap. "I can't do this."

He stopped her before she could move too much farther from him. "What is wrong?"

She gave him an incredulous look. "Do you really have to ask?"

This time, she did make it to her feet when she pulled away. She began to pace the porch straightening her clothes while she did so.

Randy sighed. "I am sorry."

She looked at him and smiled when she saw Randy had dropped his face into his hands.

He looked up. "Can you forgive me?"

"There isn't a need to. I would love to pretend I wasn't enjoying what we were doing, but I was. We were just moving too fast."

She studied him trying to gauge his reaction. He remained silent, but his eyes told her everything that she needed to know. His expression of remorse was genuine. Finally he stood up he held his hand out to her.

"You are right. We are moving too fast. Let's go for a walk."

She nodded and slipped her hand into his. They headed down the steps toward the walkway. He led the way until they reached even ground. They walked a little longer in silence. It was almost awkward, something they had never really had a problem with. It was obvious that time had passed and they were different people now. She had always been able to talk to Randy about everything—her hopes, her dreams—and he had understood them. She used to think that they shared them. It made her wonder if things could ever be the same between them.

She looked over at him giving him a shy smile. "So tell me what you have been up to for the last six years."

Randy shrugged. "Well most of it you know. After I earned my bachelor's and master's degree in criminal justice from the University of Texas, I came back home to Baxley and settled down, becoming a local police officer. I worked my way up and was promoted to chief deputy, and when David decided he was going to retire, I ran for the deputy sheriff position to replace him."

She gave him an amused look. "Well, it seems like you were successful, but then again, you always were."

He chuckled. "It looks like you have done very well yourself. If I recall correctly, you always wanted to work with children."

Her amusement faded, and she was silent. She hadn't been successful when it had come to their relationship. Neither of them had been. Randy walked away from her and went on with his life. A life they should have had together. A life that he had with someone else, and she was curious to know about it.

"And how does Wade fit into everything?"

Randy's lips curved upward. "Lila and I started dating about four years ago. The relationship moved quickly becoming hot and heavy. Lila and I had a good time together. She seemed to understand me in a way that I needed at the time."

Randy paused. "Two months into the relationship she became pregnant. Both of us wanted to get married or so I thought. We made it through the pregnancy, Wade was born, and two months later, the wedding was off and Lila was never heard from again."

Randy stopped walking. "A few months later, she signed over her parental rights."

Kristen shook her head and tried not to pass judgment, but it was difficult. She didn't know Lila, but the little she knew about her wasn't pleasant. How could a woman just walk away from her child? A child so precious she could never contemplate doing something so irrational.

"Do you know where she is?"

Randy shook his head. "Not right now. She moves around a lot, but I could find her if I needed to."

"Does it affect Wade?"

He nodded, and it was the first time she saw a look of sadness cross his face. "He wants to know why he isn't special enough to have a mom."

A sharp pain went through Kristen's chest. It was an awful thing for a child to feel the way Wade did. She was certain Randy handled the situation the best he could. It was still an awful situation to be put in.

"So what has been going on in your life for the last six years?"

Kristen chuckled. "Well, let's just say Keirra and Kayla have made it interesting. I earned my degree in elementary education and master's in child care management. This is where I ended up."

Randy chuckled. "I have heard there is more to the story."

She gave him an amused look. "So have I."

His eyebrows rose. "You asked about me?"

She smiled at his surprised expression. "Did you ask about me?"

He chuckled. "Good point, but let's head back to the house. It is getting late."

Kristen inclined her head in agreement and turned around and headed back to his parents' house. When they stepped inside, Ophelia looked up from the quilt she was working on. "Did the two of you enjoy your walk?"

Randy grinned at his mom. "Yes, we did, but it is time we get going."

Ophelia and placed her quilt aside. "Wade is upstairs asleep."

"Don't get up. I will get him."

His mother nodded and picked up her quilt, but Ophelia's eyes never left Kristen. "I never imagined I would see you in this house again after Randy told me what happened."

Kristen sat down on the couch beside Ophelia and smiled. She realized she didn't know what happened. Randy had called her and told her he wasn't interested in seeing her any longer. Still, she should have known that he would tell his mother. The only question was what had Randy told his mother? She planned to find out. Stifling a sigh of frustration, she took in her surroundings. This house held a lot of fond memories for her. Ophelia had always treated her and sisters like they were her own children.

"I sensed a change in him ever since he found out you had feelings for him. A change that went away after the two of you stopped seeing each other. A change emerged in him, and I couldn't figure out what part it was until he ran into you while enrolling Wade into your day care."

Kristen grinned, always interested in the older woman's knowledge. "What did you realize?"

"You complete him."

Kristen chuckled with disbelief, but Ophelia continued. "A part of Randy vanished when you left, and he thought he found it in Lila, but he didn't. Randy could never have with anyone else what he had with you, and I think he knows that now."

She was too shocked to respond to Ophelia's statement, and a second later, it was too late to. They both looked up when they heard Randy's footsteps on the stairs. He held a sleeping Wade in his arms. Kristen stood up. "I had a wonderful time, and thanks for dinner."

"Anytime, dear."

Randy kissed his mother on the cheek. "I will give you a call tomorrow."

"Okay. The two of you drive safe."

"We will," they replied in unison.

They walked outside of the house, and he headed to his truck and placed Wade inside of the car seat. She stood back and watched him. She always suspected Randy would make a good father. She smiled when he brushed his hand across his sleeping son's forehead.

"I had a good time tonight, Randy."

He grinned as he straightened. "Good. We can do it again sometime."

"I would like that."

He pulled her close and placed a kiss on her lips. "Good night. Drive safe."

"I will."

She turned and got into her own vehicle. She started the engine and then backed out of the driveway. When she looked in the rearview mirror, she saw Randy was close behind her. He turned off several streets prior to hers. A little while later, she turned off onto her street. She pulled up into the driveway and saw her sisters were home and, from the looks of it, were awake, although it wasn't surprising.

Since they had been back in Baxley it had been spent unpacking, fixing up their grandparent's house, and working on their own ventures. She had started her day care, and Keirra and Kayla were going to start teaching school tomorrow. It had been a busy time trying to prepare for the new steps they were taking. Kristen shut off the engine and got out of the car. She headed into the house and saw her sisters were sitting in front of the television watching Mel Gibson in *The Patriot*. After setting her purse down on the hall table, she walked over to the couch. Her sisters scooted over to make room for her, and she sat down between them.

"What are you guys still doing up?"

"We were waiting for you to get in."

She laughed knowing she had been used as an excuse for them to stay up and watch a movie. When they awoke tired, they would blame it on her.

"Thanks, I think."

"So how did it go?"

"It went very well."

Keirra frowned. "You aren't thinking about getting serious with him after all you have been through? Besides, he is a cop."

Kayla sighed. "We know that already, but you know he is a good guy."

"You are right, Kayla. Randy is a good guy. That is the only reason why I will consider giving him a second chance. He never cheated on me, never degraded me. The worst I can say about him is he broke up with me, and I have no idea why." Kristen closed her eyes. "However, I do plan on finding out why."

Her heart had been broken, and rational reasoning hadn't been a part of her thinking process at the time.

"You think so?"

"I know so."

Randy had been too good to her for it not to be the reason. Their relationship had been one of pure commitment. Neither one of them had ever sought to date other people when they were together. They had never taken their relationship lighthearted enough to disrespect each other.

"I don't know," Keirra stated with cynicism. "He made it seem final by not contacting you for six years, and let's not forget, he even moved on to another woman, got engaged, and had a baby."

Keirra had a point, and Kristen couldn't refute it. Kristen looked at both of her sisters. "Keirra is right. He told me tonight the relationship between him and Lila had been going very well and marriage was something they had both been looking forward to. They were both for the marriage."

"Yes, but was it for love or for the baby?"

Keirra snorted and rolled her eyes. "Geez, Kayla, it isn't the nineteen fifties. Men don't marry women just because they are pregnant and being chased with a shotgun."

Kristen had to fight back laughter even though it wasn't a funny statement because she knew people married for less and without a shotgun. It also made her question whether she should be giving Randy another chance. What was she going to get out of it? It was a question she didn't have an answer to right now, but she hoped that he could provide her with one. If she was going to do this she had to do it with an open mind. It was something her mother instilled in her at a young age.

"Well, I think the things that have happened in the past are neither here nor there. If I do decide to go back to Randy, it will be by my choice. Now if you two don't mind, I am going to head to bed. See you in the morning."

Her sisters told her good night, and Kristen picked up her purse and headed upstairs. Kayla and Keirra had brought up some very interesting points. Randy was a good guy, but he had moved on. She and Randy had a lot to talk about. She thought tonight was going help her figure things out. Instead she ended up with more questions.

Seeing Randy again made her realize all the feelings she had for him ten years ago still existed. They seemed to be stronger now than they had been back then. She made her way to her room undressed and put her discarded clothes in the hamper.

Her cell phone rang, and she jumped in surprise. Goodness, she was distracted but with good reason. Picking it up, she smiled when she saw Randy's number.

"Hello."

"Hey, beautiful."

She sat down on the bed. "Are you at home?"

"Yes, I am."

"I had a good time tonight."

He sighed. "So did I."

She sat there in silence before she cleared her throat. "This may sound like a strange question, but is there a particular reason you called?"

She heard the amusement in his voice when he responded. "Yes."

When he didn't continue, she laughed. It was the small things like this she had missed with Randy.

"Do you mind telling me what it is?"

"I just wanted to hear your voice," he replied softly.

She fell back onto the bed with a smile on her face. "Are you serious?"

"Yes, I am."

"Well that is very flattering."

They made small talk until Kristen cleared her throat. "Can I ask you a question, Randy?"

"Sure."

She paused, wondering if she should ask the question and how. Figuring she had nothing to lose, she went ahead and asked, "Why did you push me away like you did?"

Randy sighed with disappointment. "I was hoping we could talk about this in person, but now is a good time." He was silent for several heartbeats. "I ended our relationship because in some ways I thought you were using me for a security blanket."

She frowned, upset at the statement, and wondered how he could have thought something so wrong. "Why would you think that?"

"Well, I wanted to surprise you for graduation so I drove to Athens. When I got there, I happened to see you kissing some guy so I turned around and drove home. When you came back to Baxley for the summer, I felt like you were hanging with me because I was a sure thing. Figuring you liked the guy you were kissing, I pushed you away so that you could go back to him."

Kristen laughed when she wanted to cry. "Why didn't you ask me? Better yet, why didn't you stick around for another twenty seconds?"

It was Randy's turn to laugh. "A man does have a fragile ego, and I didn't want to see how much further it was going to go."

"Well, you would have liked the ending because it ended with me slapping him in the face. That guy you saw kissing me was a jerk and took it upon himself to make me his graduation present. I should add he didn't ask me what I thought. He just forced himself upon me."

She had shocked him by slapping him, and he had worn the mark of her slap for a while.

She paused when she grasped the reality of Randy's reason for breaking up with her. "So you ended our relationship because you thought I had fallen for another man?"

"Yes and no. I ended our relationship because I wanted to make sure you had lived your life and accomplished all of the things you wanted to accomplish. So you had the opportunity to date other people if you chose to."

Kristen closed her eyes. Six years gone because he jumped to an irrational conclusion. Six years she couldn't get back. Right now she wasn't sure she wanted them back.

"So you are telling me that you broke up with me because you *thought* I was interested in another man?"

She could hear the hesitation in Randy's voice. "I didn't know for sure but I wanted—"

She laughed harshly. "You didn't *think* to ask me either, did you, Randy?" Kristen sighed in frustration. "I can't believe you, Randy. After what we shared, all we had, you just doubted my love for you without asking for answers. Are you sure it wasn't you that wanted out?"

When he didn't respond she kept speaking. "God, Randy, you did, didn't you? You didn't want to be with me anymore so seeing another guy kissing me gave you the perfect out, didn't it?"

His silence was deafening, and anger coursed through her. She had given him the benefit of the doubt the entire time. Now she felt like a fool.

"I can't believe you. You would just throw our relationship away because you wanted out, but instead of being a man and telling me outright you use a weak excuse to end it."

"Kristen, it isn't—"

"Save it, Randy. You should have explained this six years ago. Then neither of us would be sitting here wasting our time, and I wouldn't be giving you credit for being a man that you obviously aren't."

"Kristen, I—"

"Just save it because right now I wouldn't believe anything you have to say."

Randy protested. "You don't mean that."

"How would you know? It seems as if you don't know me at all, and right now I'm not sure that I want to know you."

"Kristen, we—"

"There isn't a *we*, Randy. I'm not sure there ever was. Now I'm tired, and I'm starting to get a headache. So have a good night, and don't bother to call me again."

She disconnected the call and closed her cell phone wishing that she were on a landline so that she could slam down the receiver. Instead, she settled for slamming the cell phone down on the bed. How could Randy have done this to her? Her stomach turned, and she was sure she was going to be sick. She looked at her cell phone when it rang and knew who it was before she picked it up. Seeing Randy's name, she ignored the call. She didn't want to talk to him. Couldn't talk to him right now. To know he had been so selfish was infuriating. If he wanted to break up with her he should have just said so. It would have hurt but not as much as it did now. She spent six years thinking about a man who didn't seem to exist right now. She closed her eyes and pressed the palms of her hands to her eyes. She wouldn't cry. He wasn't worth crying over.

What she needed was a hot shower to clear her mind. Then she could go downstairs and get some ice cream. Ice cream was the best medicine to deal with a situation like this. She just hoped that her sisters weren't still up. One look at her and they would know something was wrong. Her cell phone rang again, and she growled pressing the Reject button to ignore the call. She walked into her bathroom and undressed quickly, with her mind still on her conversation with Randy. A pain shot through her heart. To know Randy didn't want to be with her after all this time was devastating. As she stepped under the spray of water, the first tear fell.

She placed her head against the wall and cried. Randy's words hurt her tonight, but everything else now made sense. It explained why he was able to move on and start a relationship with another woman. Start a family with that woman while she spent her time thinking about Randy and what went wrong. She had been such a fool. Sticking her face underneath the warm spray she resolved not to shed any more tears over Randy. He wasn't worth it. She began to bathe and wondered how she was going to pick up the pieces. A lot of her time had already been wasted on Randy, and she didn't plan on wasting anymore.

Chapter Three

"What in the world are you doing?"

Kristen stopped in the doorway to Keirra's room, and her mouth fell open. Her sister had lost her mind.

"I am rearranging my room," Keirra huffed.

Kristen shook her head and entered the room. "Why didn't you ask for some help?"

Keirra put the nightstand down where she wanted it to be before straightening up to face her sister. "Because I didn't want your help."

Kristen rolled her eyes and crossed her arms over her chest. Keirra must have had a rough day at school. She hadn't been herself all evening, but she didn't want to talk about it, so Kristen was not going to press the issue. When Keirra wanted to talk was when she would talk. She also felt as if she owed Keirra the favor because her sisters had done the same lately. The past two weeks had been stressful. It had become a full-time job to avoid Randy. Since his confession she hadn't talked to him, and she didn't plan on it. The bad thing was that Randy wasn't going away as easily as he had the first time. He called her constantly. The local florist was out of flowers, and her sisters were dying for her to tell them what happened. Through it all, she found a way to stay sane . . . barely.

She turned her attention back to her sister who was still huffing. "So is this one of those self-therapy things or do you just want a vacation?"

Keirra gave Kristen a dumbfounded look that didn't trick her at all.

"What does rearranging my room have to do with a vacation?"

"Because if you keep moving this stuff around by yourself, you are going to dislocate your back, and then you aren't going to have a choice but to take one."

Keirra stared at Kristen for several heartbeats and then a huge grin spread across her face. She started laughing so that hard tears came to her eyes, and she had to bend over to keep from falling down. Kristen wanted to remain serious about the situation but couldn't help herself, and she began to laugh. Once Kristen was able to stop laughing and catch her breath, she gave Keirra her sternest look. "Now, if you are ready to accept my help, we can get this done together."

Keirra swallowed the last of her laugh, nodding. "I would appreciate your help."

Keirra stood and told Kristen what she wanted moved and where. A short while later they had everything rearranged. Keirra thanked her, and Kristen left the room shaking her head and out of breath. This was the third time Keirra had rearranged her room. Keirra had been like this for a while now, even before their father had passed away. She could remember walking past Keirra's bedroom and watching her sister move things around in her room with their father's assistance. When she asked Keirra why she changed her room around so often, her sister had shrugged and replied she didn't like how the room looked anymore.

Kristen entered her own room wondering if her sister would ever get tired of rearranging her room all of the time. If she ever got married it would drive her husband insane, and if she had kids it would be downright ridiculous. Deep down, she already knew the answer to the question.

Sighing, she walked over to her closet, pulled out a polo work shirt and khaki shorts, and then hung them on the back of the door. She walked into her bathroom and ran water into the tub, adding her favorite bubble bath to it. Once the water was at the right level, she took off her clothes and pinned her hair up then stepped into the tub. She reached for her bathtub pillow and relaxed into the tub. She let out a long sigh and then closed her eyes. It had been a long day, and in a few hours, it was getting ready to start all over again. She relaxed letting the tension flow from her body. When her eyelids began to get heavy, she sat up and began to bathe. The last thing she needed to do was fall asleep in the tub. She made that mistake one time, and it had taken an entire bottle of lotion to make her skin presentable.

A short while later, she pulled the drain to let the water out of the tub. She wrapped a towel around her body, stopping in front of the sink. It didn't take her long to brush her teeth and braid her hair so it would be manageable in the morning. She walked into her bedroom and put on her nightgown before crawling into her bed. For some strange reason she was more tired than usual. Not that it would amaze anyone. Running around a day care after kids all day could be exhausting. Yet, she was proud of herself because she had set a goal, and after a lot of hard work, she accomplished it.

She must be more tired than she first thought because she was asleep as soon as her head hit the pillow. When her alarm went off, she groaned and swung her legs over the edge of the bed.

It was her morning to cook breakfast at the day care. The task called for her to have to get up an hour early. She went into her bathroom and brushed her teeth, then fixed stray hairs that escaped her braid overnight. It didn't take her long to get dressed. She grabbed her purse and keys, heading downstairs. The smell of coffee assailed her, and she was grateful to have Kayla for a sister. She grabbed her thermal cup and poured the coffee in it. She took an appreciative sip and then headed out the door and for her car.

Jill was waiting for her when she pulled up to the center. She took another drink of her coffee prior to climbing out of her car. Jill met her at the front door with a smile.

"Is it early enough for you?"

Unlocking the door, Kristen rolled her eyes at Jill. Sometimes she wanted to hit Jill for being so positive, but there were times when it came in handy. Jill followed her inside and locked the door behind her. It would be at least thirty minutes until the first child arrived. It was all the time they needed to make sure everything needed for the day was ready. Once it was, she and Jill began making preparations for breakfast. They had to make sure the children that were going to ride the bus to school had breakfast. It was a service she provided because the bus picked up the children late in the morning, and by the time they got off the bus they had just enough time to get to class. Once all of the school kids were off things were a lot less hectic. She had the chance to break away and try to complete some paperwork.

Zebbie stuck her head in the office. "Randy just dropped Wade off."

Kristen rolled her eyes in agitation. Her staff had followed this routine since they found out she wasn't speaking to Randy.

"You don't have to announce when Randy drops Wade off everyday."

Zebbie gave her a look of disbelief. "Are you sure? It seems like you disappear into your office and close the door at least five minutes before Randy is scheduled to drop Wade off."

Kristen felt her mouth drop open. "I do not."

Zebbie nodded. "Yes, you do, and everyone has noticed."

Zebbie stepped farther into the office. "The only thing I will say is that you can't avoid Randy forever. At some point, you will have to talk to him about whatever it is you are mad at him about."

Kristen put down her pen and dropped her face into her hands. "I wish it were that simple."

Zebbie exhaled softly. "It is as simple as you make it, and if it makes you feel any better Randy looks worse than you do."

Kristen smiled as Zebbie left her office. She was happy to hear Randy was having as hard of a time as she was. Since he had revealed why he had broken up with her, she had experienced an abundance of emotions. Right now, anger and disbelief were the two she had a hard time controlling. What had she done to deserve such callousness? There was work to be done, and she didn't have time to go over the things that could have been with Randy. Picking up her pen, she tried to focus on the paper in front of her. A short time later, she sighed with frustration and put her pen down. It was obvious that she wasn't going to get any more paperwork done. Her mind was on Randy, and once that happened, her concentration was gone. There was no use in sitting there pretending it hadn't. She stood up and left her office. Zebbie had the children engrossed in story time. They had story-time three times a day. It kept the kids preoccupied, and it got them interested in reading. She heard Zebbie say, "The end," and smiled.

"All right, children. It is class time."

Everyone got up full of excitement. She led her four-year-olds to their area and stopped to check in on Jill on the way. Each of them had an age group to take care of. Jill had two infants, one seven-month-old, and one ten-month-old. She also had two one-year-olds. Zebbie had five two-year-olds and one three-year-old, Wade. He liked Zebbie and was always well behaved with her. To be truthful, he was well behaved with everyone. He was also Zebbie's little helper. When they combined all of the children together, the two-year-olds followed him around and tried to do everything he did. It was funny to watch at times. With all the age groups being accounted for, it left her with the four-year-olds, and she had six of them. Gerri rotated out with whoever needed a break until the school-age children, who were her responsibility, came in. So far, things were working out okay with the way the system had been arranged, but she was looking at bringing in two more workers. She needed a cook and another attendant. Although she could consider three additional workers, there were days when they needed a full-time receptionist.

It would be helpful to have someone who was able to stay at the front desk the entire time the children were being dropped off and picked up. The day care had grown larger than she ever imagined in the short amount of time that passed since she opened. At least this part of her life had worked out. She always thought she would be married to Randy by now, possibly with a few children of their own, while she ran the successful day care. Well at least she had achieved part of the plan. Quicker than she expected and now it was past time to hire some extra help. She had hoped to finish the advertisement for the positions before lunch. It was obvious she wasn't going to. After they made it through the first lesson it was going to be lunchtime, and they would get busier from there. She would be finishing her work from home. When she considered how much thoughts of Randy preoccupied her mind when she was at home, keeping busy might be a good idea.

Once the children were situated, they began working on the alphabet. They reviewed the letters they had covered so far them moved onto the letter Q. It was the letter of the alphabet they were going to focus on all week. She was amused when she asked her students to give her a word with the letter Q. Bobby called out the word *quiet,* and everyone took him literally. After a quick laugh, she was able to get the group to give her a few more words. She supplied them with a few more. By the time they finished the lesson, it was lunchtime. She walked into the kitchen and looked at Jill. One thing she knew for certain was she needed to get the advertisement for the job postings completed tonight. Otherwise they were going to have to start joining the children for naptime.

Chapter Four

Kristen looked over at Keirra when she began to whine. She sounded like one of her children at the day care. It was a sound that shouldn't come from a grown woman. Keirra had been complaining and making all sorts of noises for about twenty minutes. Kristen found herself rolling her eyes at her sister's antics before speaking.

"Whining isn't going to help, Keirra."

They were supposed to be shopping at Mandi's, but so far, Keirra was more focused on food than clothes. She looked up to see if Mandi had come from the back yet, but she hadn't. Mandi had been a year behind them in school, but she had been creative in fashion even back then so it was no surprise she owned a clothing store now.

"But I am hungry," Keirra complained.

Kayla shook her head, unable to believe her grown sister had resorted to such tactics. "No, you aren't. You just want Sam's Café because you're a glutton and it's close by."

Kristen almost laughed at the expression on Keirra's face. "Tell you what. You can go over to Sam's Café and eat while Kayla and I finish shopping."

"But that would mean I would have to eat by myself."

"You could invite Darren along. I am sure he wouldn't mind accompanying you," Kayla said. The statement earned her another roll of the eyes from Keirra and laughter from Kristen. Darren was Keirra's high school prom date, and he seemed to be happy that Keirra was back in Baxley.

"You are so not funny, Kayla."

Kristen laughed under her breath as she looked at the clothes on the rack. Most of the items in the store were creations Mandi had designed. Amusement spread across her face as she admired the clothing.

"Well, I was wondering when you were going to come in and see me."

All three of them turned at the sound of Mandi's voice. She still looked the same with the exception of the sparkling gold diamond ring on her left hand. They each hugged her and congratulated her on her marriage and the store.

"I'd heard the three of you were back in town, but I have been so busy I haven't had time to get by and see you."

Kristen shook her head. "Don't worry about it. Trust us, we understand what it is like to be busy."

Mandi linked arms with her. "You are just the person I need to talk to."

"I heard you have a day care center, and I have three children I would love to enroll."

Kristen fought to keep a straight face. Mandi didn't look like she was the mother of three children. It seemed she had been busy since high school.

"Come by first thing Monday morning, and we can talk."

Mandi nodded. "I will be there. Now take a look around, and let me know if you need my help with anything."

Kristen smiled and rejoined her sisters. They had always liked her advice when it came to shopping. Kayla had once told her she was jealous that somehow she always managed to look like she stepped off the cover of a fashion magazine. Even though they shopped at the same place, they always managed to have a different look.

Kristen tended to gravitate more toward the feminine-yet-modern-chic look, always wearing some shade of pink and a skirt. Keirra had more of the casual look mixed with a little athletic flare, always wearing jeans or khaki pants with a sweater, casual blouse or T-shirt. Kayla went for the professional look for the most part. She was always wearing nice slacks or skirts with a nice blouse or shirt. She was pretty certain Kayla owned three pairs of jeans at the most, complaining that she didn't like how restrictive they were. Even though this was the case, there were always times when they strayed from the norm. Kristen had a way of putting outfits together for them to bring out the best look.

Kristen looked down at the two shirts that she held and grinned. "I think I have everything I want."

Kayla put a shirt back on the rack. "I am right behind you."

"Thank goodness," Keirra called out in relief.

"It doesn't mean we're going to go to Sam's," Kristen teased.

Keirra turned to face them. "Oh, you two can be such pains in the ass."

Kayla smirked. "I would rather have a pain in my ass than weight on it."

It was Keirra's turn to roll her eyes. "Oh, please, you run a mile or two every day."

"Yes, I would like it if I didn't have to make it three or four."

Kristen laughed. "Give it up, Keirra. You—" Her cell phone rang cutting her off. She frowned when she saw Randy's number. She looked at her sisters. "It's Randy."

Keirra rolled her eyes while Kayla gave her a pointed look. "Are you going to answer it?"

Kristen shook her head at Kayla. "No, I'm not ready to talk to him yet."

Kayla sighed with exasperation. "Your obsession with avoidance isn't going to help in this situation."

She gave Kayla a warning look. "I don't have—"

Her phone rang again, cutting her off, but it was a text message. She groaned, opening the message. Scanning it, she gasped. She hit the button to redial Randy's number. When he answered, she sighed. "I hope this isn't an attempt to get me to talk to you."

She heard him exhale softly. "No, it isn't. Mr. Feldon had a heart attack."

She almost dropped the phone. "When? Is he okay?"

Her sisters interrupted at her horrified expression.

"What is it?" Kayla asked.

"Is it Wade?" Keirra added.

She shook her head at her sisters. "Hang on a second, Randy. No, it's Mr. Feldon. Randy said he has had a heart attack."

Her sisters gasped. Kirsten and her sisters had spent a lot of time in his office, and most of the time, they hadn't been in trouble. Outside the few times when they had been in trouble and deserved to be in the office, they had gone to him in need of advice—fatherly advice they couldn't get anywhere else, and Mr. Feldon had been happy to give it when he could. If he couldn't give them advice, he had always led them in the direction of someone who could. Because of that, they had always appreciated him. Up until a year ago they had maintained very regular contact with him. After that it seemed like everyone had been swept up in their respective lives, and they had lost contact.

While she got the rest of information from Randy, she was in search of Mandi. When she found her, she and her sisters dumped their clothes into her hands.

"Mandi, is there any way you can hold these items for us? We need to get to the hospital."

Mandi looked at them with concern. "Is everything okay?"

Kristen shook her head. "No. Mr. Feldon has had a heart attack."

Mandi's eyes widened in shock. "Is he okay?"

Kristen shrugged. "We have no idea, but we'll let you know when we find out."

Mandi nodded and took the clothes out of their hands. "Please let me know what is going on."

Kristen led the way out of the store. They made their way to Kayla's car, and she drove them all to the hospital. Once they arrived she realized the Baxley community hospital had been expanded upon a lot since they had left. It now had a Trauma unit and ICU.

Randy was waiting outside the entrance for them. He gave her a brief look before greeting Kayla and Keirra. Zebbie was right. Randy did look as if he were suffering. She closed her eyes. Now wasn't the time to think about the problems she had with Randy. Instead, she wanted to see Mr. Feldon. Opening her eyes, she looked at Randy. "How did you know Mr. Feldon a heart attack?"

He gave her a small smile. "I heard the emergency call on my radio." They stepped onto the elevator, and he pressed the button to the floor they needed to be on. "I have just spoken with the doctor who stated he only had a mild heart attack, but he needs to take it easy from here on out."

The elevator sounded out to let them know they had arrived on their floor. They stepped out and Randy led them toward the ICU. He spoke when the nurses acknowledged him as they walked to Mr. Feldon's room. A nurse was coming out of the room. Randy stopped her.

"How is he doing?"

The nurse's expression was reassuring. "He is doing much better. We're getting ready to move him down to a regular room. We are going to keep him over night."

Randy nodded, and the nurse continued on. They entered the room, and Mr. Feldon opened his eyes. Mr. Feldon had aged well, but he looked tired. Kristen was the first to approach the bed, and he grinned.

"I'd heard you ladies were back in town. I just wish I was in better shape for your company."

She leaned down and gave Mr. Feldon a kiss on the cheek. "It would help if you took better care of yourself."

He smiled when she straightened up. "I do the best I can."

She took a seat on the edge of the bed when Kayla came over. "Well, I guess you need some assistance."

Mr. Feldon laughed. "And I am sure you are more than willing to help."

Keirra was the last to come forward. "Just like you were willing to help us when we needed it."

Kristen stared at Mr. Feldon with appreciation for everything he had done for her and her sisters.

Sitting here on the edge of his hospital bed, Kristen hated the lapse in communication. "Is there anyone you need for us to call?"

He shook his head. "I have already called my family, and a few people should be here sometime tonight or in the morning." Mr. Feldon smiled, and he reached out and squeezed her hand. "I thank you for coming to see me."

"You are more than welcome, and we will come by tomorrow just to check on you."

Keirra's expression was stern when she looked at Mr. Feldon. "And we won't have any argument from you."

Mr. Feldon laughed but it was cut short when he grabbed his chest. When they went to call for the nurse he waved them off. "I am okay. I just laughed at little too hard."

Kristen placed a hand on his arm. "You must try not to overdo it, Mr. Feldon."

He chuckled. "I don't know. With you girls around, it might be hard to do."

Kayla rolled her eyes. "I can guarantee you our wild days are over, Mr. Feldon."

His expression was pure humor. "I would hope not. You ladies are too young not to have a few wild days left in you."

Kristen felt her eyes widen. "Mr. Feldon, I can't believe you said that to us."

The older gentleman closed his eyes. "It is okay. You all are human. You ought to know it by now."

Kayla leaned down and placed another kiss on Mr. Feldon's cheek. "Trust me when I say we are, but we are going to go so you can get some rest."

Keirra was next. "We will leave our number at the nurse's station. Have them give us a call if you need anything."

"I will do, but before you go, I would like to talk to Kristen alone."

She looked at Mr. Feldon in surprise but nodded in agreement. Randy shook his hand, and then left the room. Keirra and Kayla said good-bye and left the room as well. With the room clear, she turned to look at him. "What did you want to talk to me about?"

He smiled at her. "I am glad to see you and your sisters are back in town. I have been meaning to come by and see you guys."

Kristen's lips curved upward in amusement. "And we should have come by to see you. I have to admit my sisters and I have been busy, but it's no excuse."

Mr. Feldon's hand came up to touch hers. "That isn't what I wanted to talk to you about. I wanted to talk to you about Randy."

She gave him a puzzled look. "Why do you need to talk to me about Randy?"

His smiled faded. "Because word has it that the two of you are fighting the attraction that you have for each other."

Kristen sighed. "Mr. Feldon—"

He gave her a knowing look. "I know, but let me say this because it needs to be said. I see myself in him. I have for a while. It has only gotten worse since he had Wade."

Kristen laughed, but it was more out of necessity than out of humor. "Well, Mr. Feldon, knowing you like I do, I can't say it's a bad thing."

He shook his head. "I'm not talking about his character. I am talking about his ability to be open to a relationship." Mr. Feldon sighed. "Randy has changed a lot since you two stopped seeing each other. Lila did a number on him. She hurt him, and he is just now becoming the Randy we all once knew again." A sad expression appeared on his face. "I am speaking from experience. My ex-wife did a number on me, too, so much so I never married again. Not because I didn't meet anyone worth marrying, but because I couldn't let go of the past." Mr. Feldon reached out and took her hand in his. "I look into Randy's eyes, and I know he hasn't let the past go. I don't think he will until someone comes along and forces him to."

Kristen closed her eyes in sadness. "Mr. Feldon, I can't imagine what Randy went through, but I'm not over the past either. I'm not even sure what our past was. What am I supposed to do when it seems like Randy didn't want to be with me in the first place?"

He looked at her in shock. "Why would you say that? Everyone knows that

Randy was head over heels for you."

Kristen's laugh was devoid of humor. "I thought so as well, but not anymore. Mr. Feldon, Randy broke up with me because he didn't want to be with me anymore."

Mr. Feldon stared at her with utter disbelief. "Did Randy tell you that?"

Kristen paused. He hadn't said it outright, but she was smart enough to read between the lines. Randy hadn't denied the accusation. Then again, she hadn't given him much chance to. Was there more to this?

"Kristen, I can't tell you what to do, but I think that you should at least give Randy the chance to explain. With the history the two of you have together, both of you deserve it. I know for sure there is one person Randy will talk to if she is willing to listen."

He stopped speaking. It was obvious he had more to say, but he didn't. She could tell by his expression he thought she was the person Randy would talk to.

The truth was that she and Randy did need to talk about their relationship. That was the problem. She and Randy never discussed their relationship. They talked about everything else, including the personal goals that they had but never their future together. Could that be the reason why Randy reacted the way he had when he saw her with another man? She groaned when she realized that Mr. Feldon had given her more questions than answers. Since her blow up with Randy, she had done a lot of thinking about it. Was she prepared to spend the rest of her life without Randy? One thing she knew for certain was that Mr. Feldon was right. She had to talk to Randy, and she hoped she was prepared for the outcome.

* * * *

"Are you sure that you want to do this?"

Kristen stared at Kayla in the mirror. She was getting ready to meet Randy at Sam's Café. After her conversation with Mr. Feldon she could no longer put off the inevitable. Avoiding Randy was starting to affect her health. She suffered from a lack of sleep and concentration. Meeting in a public place would mean that she would have to be rational and not scream at him like she wanted to. She knew that screaming wasn't going to solve anything at this point. She wasn't sure if anything would.

"No, Kayla. I'm not sure that I want to do this, but I have to. As much as I would like to deny it, I'm still attracted to Randy, and I'm tired of fighting it."

Kayla reached out and squeezed her shoulder. "I know that you still care about Randy. Just make sure that you do what is best for you."

Kristen nodded. "I will. Thank you, Kayla."

Her sister left the bathroom, and Kristen twisted her hair up into large clip. She took one last look at her reflection in the mirror and, releasing a deep breath, tried to force the tension from her body. A short time later, she was walking out the front door. She made the quick drive to Sam's Café and saw that Randy's car was already there. She took another deep breath and released it slowly as he got out of the car. Her nerves were racing, and she couldn't remember being this nervous since the first time she had been alone with Randy.

Randy had been in the garage working on his car, and his sister, Emily, had been helping him. Emily had spotted Kristen and called her over to the house. Emily had borrowed a pair of Keirra's shoes and wanted to return them. Once the shoes had been deposited into her hands, Kristen turned to go only to be stopped in her tracks by the sight of a now shirtless Randy. She had tried to avert her eyes before he saw her, but she must have been a second too late. Randy had called her over, and it seemed to be the longest walk of her life. When she saw the cherry-red convertible, she smiled. The first thought that had come to mind was it was the perfect car for Keirra. He asked her if she liked his car, and once she gave him a mindless nod, he had given her a rundown of the car.

She had just stood there nodding repeatedly like a bobble head doll. The next thing she knew, his lips had come down on hers. It was the first time she had been kissed. She had been so shocked that she had pulled back, and the next thing she could remember was running all the way home, but she hadn't gone into the house until she had calmed down.

Keirra and Kayla had still known something had been wrong, but she hadn't confided in them until Randy had shown up on their porch with a teddy bear in his hands. They had gone for a drive, and he confessed his feelings for her. He had also told her he was going to wait for her, and if she felt the same to wait for him. She had been flattered beyond belief, and she had waited for him. They had corresponded the rest of the school year until he returned home for the summer. It wasn't until he asked her out on a date to celebrate her eighteenth birthday that it officially became a relationship. A relationship that lasted for four years, and it had been a wonderful relationship—until it fell apart. Now she wanted that back, but when she walked into Sam's Café, she wondered if they could ever regain what they had lost.

She paused when she saw Randy stand up in a back corner. The restaurant wasn't full, but he was sitting at a table that offered them maximum privacy, a detail she was thankful for. The things she wanted to say to Randy were meant for his ears only. He remained standing, surprising her when he presented her with a bouquet of lilies. She accepted the flowers graciously.

"Thank you," she murmured as he held out her chair.

She studied him across the table, and he gave her a hesitant smile.

"I hope you don't mind, but I ordered for you. This way we can eat and talk without too many interruptions."

She gave a quick nod. "That is fine."

Randy knew her well enough to know what she liked, and it gave her the ability to get to the point of dinner. The lemonade sitting in front of her was proof of that. She glanced at the flowers and then looked back at Randy. He looked as tired as she felt, but he was still handsome. She was quickly reminded why she fell in love with him the first time around. She blinked when Randy cleared his throat.

"If it's okay, I would like to start."

She gave him a quick nod. "Okay."

He studied her several heartbeats before speaking. "I'm sorry, Kristen. Due to my stupidity, insecurity, or whatever you want to call it, I made a mistake that I can never take back."

She stared at him for a long time before responding. "How could you think that about me, Randy? How could you just be so willing to automatically assume the worst of me?"

He gave her a horrified look. "That wasn't what I meant to do."

"But it's what you did," she stated softly. "You doubted everything about me, everything about us with one simple action. What would make you do something like that?"

He made a sound of frustration. "Stupidity to begin with, but the main thing was insecurity. We never talked about our plans together. I talked about what I wanted to do with my future, and you talked about what you wanted in yours, but we never talked about our future. When I saw you kissing that guy, I wasn't sure that we had one so I thought I would do both of us a favor and walk away."

Kristen closed her eyes and shook her head. Randy had a good point. The same exact thing had crossed her mind, only it was six years later. During their relationship, she had been so comfortable with it that she had just assumed it would work out.

"I thought that we would always be together, Randy. I just assumed it would be automatically. To me everything happened so naturally that I didn't think we needed to talk about it. I guess I was too secure in what we had."

He reached across the table and took her hand in his. "No, Kristen, this was me. This is all on me. It isn't your fault I gave up so easy. I have always wanted you. I always thought we would be together."

He paused. "It didn't take me long to realize that I made a mistake, but I was too embarrassed to come crawling back. I wasn't sure that you would take me back if I did."

She pulled her hand out of his embrace. "What makes you think that I will now?"

She watched as an expression of remorse became visible on his face. "I don't, and I wouldn't blame you if you didn't, but I am hoping that you will at least give me a chance. I made the mistake once of not trying to get you back. It isn't a mistake that I will make again."

"Why was it so easy for you to move on?"

He gave her a stunned look but was unable to respond as their food was delivered to the table. As soon as they were alone again he spoke. "*Easy?* Being without you was never easy, but I made a decision, and I had to live with it."

She gave him a pointed look. "What about Lila?"

"I cared for Lila, although not in the way I thought I did now when I look back. I might regret the relationship, but I don't regret Wade."

She hated that because there had been no one else since Randy, he had been the only man for her whether she wanted to admit it or not. There was another round of silence before Kristen spoke. "So where do we go from here, Randy?"

He gave her a look of uncertainty. "I don't know. A lot has changed, but I know I want to try, and I'm hoping you do as well."

She gave him a sad look. "You are right. A lot has changed. Do you think it is possible for us to be together again and it be like it was?"

"I don't know, Kristen, but tonight was the first step, and I would love to see you again next weekend. I have Saturday off, but I am on call."

Kristen stifled a groan. She wasn't ready to say no, but she wasn't ready to say yes either. This wasn't going to be easy, and she knew that Randy wasn't going to make it any easier either. She studied him across the table and looked for any hint that he was being dishonest, and she couldn't find any.

"It's not going to be that easy, Randy. You didn't have any reason not to trust me, but you have given me plenty of reason not to trust you. I just need time to think about this. Right now that is all that I can promise you."

She expected Randy to press the issue, but he didn't. Instead, he gave her a small smile. "That is all I can ask for, Kristen."

She looked down at her chicken Alfredo and tried to focus on the conversation while she ate, but when she finally arrived home she could hardly remember any of it. Her mind was on why she could come up with more reasons to give Randy a second chance than reasons why she shouldn't.

* * * *

Randy climbed into his truck and drove the short distance to his parents' house, his mind on Kristen the entire way. Dinner with Kristen hadn't gone the way he planned, but she hadn't said no. Her answer gave him hope. He wanted another chance with Kristen to build the life they should already have. He had been stupid to push her away without talking to her first. However, he wouldn't be the first to claim emotional maturity at the age of twenty-six. Yet, six years could make a difference. At the age of thirty-two, he was certain of what he wanted. He wanted Kristen and hoped she would give him the opportunity to prove it.

He grinned when he pulled into his parent's driveway. Wade was out in the front yard playing. His mother was in her garden checking on her plants. Wade began jumping up and down when he saw him. Randy stepped out and scooped his son up into his arms.

"Did you have a good time?" he asked Wade as he walked toward the house.

His mother stood as he walked toward her. Stretching upward she placed a kiss on her son's cheek. "Glad to see you made it."

He glanced at his watch. "Am I late?"

His mother shook her head. "No, you are earlier than I thought you would be, but from your expression and the smile that hasn't left your face, I can guess why."

Randy realized he was grinning, but he was happy. Kristen hadn't said she would give him a chance, but the fact that she was thinking about it was enough for him.

His mother turned and led the way into the house. "So things are okay between you and Kristen?"

He put Wade down before answering his mother. "Yes and no. She didn't say yes, but she didn't scream at me either. She needs time to think about it, and I am willing to give it to her."

His mother nodded. "I always did like Kristen. She is good for you. She also seems to be good for Wade. I have noticed some good changes in him."

Wade looked over at his son who was gathering up his toys. His son did seem a lot happier.

"So are you prepared to do whatever it takes?"

He turned back to his mother with surprise. "What do you mean?"

"I mean that you need to understand that Kristen was hurt by you. Equate it to how hurt you felt after Lila ended your relationship as abruptly as she did."

Randy sighed, not wanting to think about how devastated he had been. If it hadn't been for Wade and his parents, he might not have recovered as quickly as he did.

"What do you suggest I do, Mom?"

His mother gave him a sympathetic look. "There is nothing you can do but give Kristen time. She will let you know when she is ready." His mother smiled. "But it wouldn't hurt for you to show her what she is missing out on in the mean time."

He thought about what his mother said as he helped Wade put his toys in the bag before telling his mother bye. Wade climbed into the truck, and Randy strapped him into his car seat. As he backed out of the driveway, he realized his mother was right. He couldn't sit back and wait for Kristen to make the decision all by herself. He had to come up with a plan to show her why she should do more than just think about giving him a chance.

Chapter Five

Kristen groaned as she pulled into the driveway. Even though it was still early she had hoped her sisters wouldn't still be up. After dinner with Randy, she needed time to think. She sighed in frustration as she got out of the car. There would be no chance of that. She opened the door and both of her sisters looked up at her.

"How was the date?"

Kristen rolled her eyes at Kayla. "It wasn't a date."

Kayla frowned. "Did you sit down at a restaurant, eat, and have conversation?"

Kristen groaned. "Yes."

Kayla smiled. "Sounds like a date to me."

Kristen flopped down on the couch. "Now is not the time for your sense of humor, Kayla."

Keirra sat up and turned the volume down on the television. "So it seems like everything went well."

"Everything went perfectly," Kristen half growled.

"Damn cops," Keirra grumbled before going into a tirade of cursing cops and sisters too weak to resist them. Kristen laughed at her sisters and shook her head.

"Look, you two, I appreciate your concern, but I am a capable of handling this right now. If I can't, I will let you know."

This was hers and hers alone. What she had experienced with Randy was wonderful, and she wouldn't change it for anything. Still, she had to figure out what it was she had with Randy. There was no doubt she still had feeling for him, but what was she going to do about it? Getting involved with Randy again was a major risk to her heart. There was a lot of thinking to be done and decisions to be made. He had pushed her away once, and six years had been lost because of it. They both had changed, yet a lot of things were still the same. Kristen looked over at her sisters. Keirra was still staring her down, and Kayla was still smiling, but they were respecting her wishes and not cornering her for an inquisition. She would have to keep that in mind when her sisters found romance.

Keirra and Kayla had dated their share, but when she thought about it neither one of them had ever had a serious boyfriend. Not like she had been with Randy. Keirra had never gone out with anyone long enough for him to be classified as a boyfriend.

The three of them had their quirks men just couldn't get around. She was considered to be the shy one, the non-confrontational one, but normally, she scared men off with her strong sense of feminism. Men knew that when she was with them, it was because she wanted to be with them in return and not because she needed to be. Kayla was the perfectionist and always had the perfect amount of rationale. If that didn't run a man off, her brain did. Keirra was athletic and a little bit of a control freak. She tended to be opinionated and outspoken, which left men without a word to say because they couldn't get a word in if they wanted to. The three of them together made a hell of a trio. It also made for interesting times. People always worried about twins switching places. Well, triplets liked to play the switching game, too, and they did it a little better.

There had been the time in high school when she had been required to give a speech in front of the class and she had been terrified so Kayla had taken her place. She felt bad about the situation, but she couldn't have done it herself. The interesting thing was to this day she still was not good at speaking in front of people, but she could do it now thanks to her college years.

There had also been the time Kayla had to complete an activity course in P. E. class, and Keirra had taken her place. Kristen had come in handy when Keirra had been running late to basketball practice. She filled in long enough to say she was present, and that had been it. They had gotten into some sticky situations, but their teamwork had pulled them through.

Kristen yawned and realized she was sleepy. It had been a long weekend. Standing up, she moaned as she felt her muscles protest. "It's bedtime for me."

Kayla nodded. "It is getting late. We should be going to bed."

"Speak for yourself," Keirra grumbled.

She stood before walking over to each of her sisters' and kissed both of them on their cheeks. "I love you guys. Good night."

They reciprocated, and she walked out of the living. She realized just how tired she was when she started up the stairs. Once she made it to her room, she took a quick shower and crawled into bed. She reached for her favorite teddy bear and squeezed it tight in her arms. The bear was scruffy looking with good reason. It was the same one that Randy gave her the day he kissed her for the first time. She smiled at the memory. She closed her eyes and soon she was fast asleep.

* * * *

It seemed like she had just closed her eyes when the alarm went off. She brought a hand down on the buzzer and got out of bed. After she arrived at work, the day seemed to fly by. She locked up her day care center and hopped into her car. The drive home was short, and when she walked into the house, she sniffed the air to try to guess what was for dinner. Her sisters came out of the kitchen, and they looked ready to go out. She gave them a questioning look.

"What is for dinner?"

Kayla grinned. "Sam's Café."

A smile came to Kristen's face, and she headed for the stairs. "Give me fifteen minutes, and I will be ready."

She loved Sam's Café. Sam's offered a little of everything from Tex-Mex to Italian and everything in between. She went into her room and hopped around shedding clothing until she was naked. Her next stop was to the shower, and she made it quick. When she stepped out of the shower, she dried off, went to her closet, and began flipping through her clothes to find out what she was going to wear. She decided on her powder pink top. It was an asymmetrical bandana top. She had several of the tops in several colors, but the pink one was her favorite. She added her blue jean skirt, which stopped a few inches above her knees, and topped it off with the pink calf-height boots she had bought with the top.

She put her clothes on in record time. The next battle was going to be making the decision on how she wanted to style her hair. She decided to keep it simple. After parting her hair down the middle, she plaited a braid on each side. When she was done, she placed a pink beret-style hat on her head. While spraying perfume, she gave herself a once-over and, satisfied, walked out of her room and down the stairs.

Her sisters were standing downstairs waiting for her. Keirra glanced down at her watch and smiled. "You made it with a minute to spare, and you still look great."

Kristen laughed. "Whose vehicle are we going in?"

Kayla spoke up. "We can go in mine."

The three grabbed their purses and headed out the front door. Keirra locked the house up, and they were on their way. Kayla drove into town, and a short time, they pulled in front of Sam's Café. They had been back to the café a handful of times since they had come back to town. They climbed out of Kayla's vehicle and stepped into the café. Kristen was glad that it wasn't crowded and that they were seated quickly.

After they placed their drink orders, all eyes went to Kayla. Kristen leaned closer to Kayla. "So how was your date with Richard?"

She shrugged. "It was a date, but he has changed a lot."

Keirra nodded. "He seems a lot more attractive now than he was in high school."

Kristen laughed. "Most of us tend to be."

Kayla grinned. "You know what they say."

Keirra rolled her eyes. "No, I don't, but I am sure you are going to tell me."

Kayla shrugged. "Of course I am. They say everything gets better with age."

Keirra just shook her head. "Whoever said that never heard of perishable foods."

Kristen almost choked on her drink at her sister's cynicism, but she managed to laugh instead. "Kayla, I think you said it wrong. I think it goes something like he has aged like a fine wine."

Kayla pondered the correction before shrugging. "You could be right. The bottom line is the man looks good."

Kristen nodded. "There are a lot of people around town we haven't seen."

Kayla scoffed. "Yeah, well, there are a lot of people I have run into that I would have loved to avoid but couldn't."

Kristen gave Kayla a confused look. "What are you talking about?"

"I had a little run-in with Michelle, Margaret, and Trish."

Kristen groaned at the mention of those three names. The three women were mean to the core. They always had been. They were all the same age as Randy, but for some reason, they had always been in competition with her and her sisters and had been a pain in the butt from day one. It had made times in Baxley a little difficult to say the least. "What happened?"

Kayla laughed. "What hasn't happened? This has been going on since the beginning of the school year. I was fortunate enough to get all three of their daughters in my class."

Kristen's eyes widened. "Well, you forgot to mention that part."

Kayla shrugged. "There was no need to. The girls are just like their mothers, but they haven't given me any problems. At least, up until today I didn't have any problems."

Kristen gave her sister a questioning look. "Do you think there will be a problem now?"

Kayla smirked. "I'm sure it's due to the other exciting event that occurred."

"And that would be?"

"Brigette enrolled Somer into my class today. She wasn't doing well in class with the other English teacher. Brigette is hoping I can change Somer's behavioral issues."

Kristen felt a smile come to her face at the mention of Brigette Holbrock's name. She was a good person, one of the first people to befriend them when they first moved to Baxley, even though she was four years older than them. She had lived on what was known as the poor side of town, but it hadn't concerned her or her sisters. Brigette was a sweet person who had a rough time in life but had dealt with it a lot better than most.

"Is everything okay with Somer?"

Kayla grinned. "I had to prove to her that I am smarter than her and qualified to teach her, and she was fine."

Kristen and Keirra laughed. "How long did it take?"

Kayla rolled her eyes at Keirra. "Ten minutes."

Picking up her menu, Kristen shook her head. "Sometimes I wonder why I even torture myself with talking to you guys."

Keirra smiled. "Because you love us."

Kayla rolled her eyes. "When it comes to you, trust me, it's out of necessity."

Kristen laughed again. She loved her sisters and didn't know what she would do without them. Her sisters picked up their menus and tried to decide what they were going to eat.

* * * *

"Damn."

Randy looked up in surprise after Eric let the word of profanity slip. This was the guy he wanted to be his next deputy. He was showing Eric around the town to show him what he would be getting himself into. He turned to look in the direction Eric was looking in, and he grinned when he saw the Smith Triplets, although he felt like he had been punched in the gut when he got a full look at Kristen. She was sexy as hell. Even though it had been less than twenty-four hours since he last saw her, he missed her. She said that she needed time, but it didn't mean that he should sit around until she made up her mind. Like his mother stated, he needed to provide her with extra motivation. Not being able to resist, he took the last swig of his coffee and sat the cup down. He pulled out his wallet and placed a few bills on the table. It was enough to cover his and Eric's food plus a nice tip. He stood up.

"I will introduce you."

Eric grinned. "Well, if you insist."

Randy shook his head. He liked the guy and could see him fitting in well in Baxley.

He headed over to a table where the trio was sitting, with Eric following right behind him. Kristen was sitting facing him. When she saw him, a look of shock crossed her face. She cleared the expression but not fast enough for him not to see it. He smiled. Kristen was more affected by him than she wanted to admit. When he reached the table, he noticed Kayla was busy studying her menu and Keirra was digging around in her purse.

"Good evening, ladies. Do you mind if we join you?"

Kristen hesitated briefly before sliding over to make room for him. He grinned at Keirra when she looked up from the menu, and she froze. Not being a stranger to sexual attraction, he could tell Keirra was attracted to Eric as well. He chuckled under his breath when Kayla nudged Keirra to encourage her to move over. He watched Keirra regain her composure then slide over. He gave the introductions after Eric sat down.

"This is Eric Brooks, a candidate for the vacant deputy position."

His eyes widened when Keirra began to choke on a sip of soda. She turned and gave him a hard look. He looked at Kayla, who gave a quick shake of her head. He looked back at Keirra, who was still glaring at him. He sighed, looking over at Kristen. Her attention had been directed to the menu in front of her. He smiled when he saw the slight tremor in her hand. Pursuing Kristen might be more fun than he thought it would be.

Chapter Six

"What do you want to eat?"

Kristen glanced at the menu before looking up at Randy. "I will take the chicken marinara."

Randy nodded. "Anything else?"

She shook her head, and when their waiter came up to the table, he placed their order. It was their first official date. So far, everything was going okay.

She had been shocked when he sent a large bouquet of orchids to the day care with an apology for having to cancel their dinner plans for the night and asking her to join him another night. Gerri and Zebbie had teased her, telling her that she would be crazy to turn down the invitation. She let the two of them worry when she pretended to ponder the invitation she already planned to accept before putting them out of their misery, and she called Randy to accept his invite to join him for dinner. She could no longer fight her attraction to him. She wasn't sure she wanted to.

It ended up being a forty-eight hour rain check, and now as she sat across from him, she was glad she had the opportunity to see him this week. Even though it was only Wednesday, she knew he had conducted quite a few interviews. He looked tired, and she reached across the table and touched his hand. She was deeply moved that he no longer wanted to put the date off but not at the expense of his rest.

"We can take the food to go if you want to."

He smiled and shook his head. "No, I have always enjoyed taking you out, and I have been looking forward to this. It won't kill me to stay up another hour or two. Not for you."

The waiter came back to the table with their food, and they caught up on old times laughing at the good memories they shared. Some of her fondest memories existed right here at Sam's Café. She didn't know what it was about the small, family-run restaurant, but something appealed to her, her sisters, and Randy. A lot of their dates had been here. She could remember squeezing into the booths together and eating off of each other's plates if they weren't feeding each other.

They finished their meal, and she declined dessert when he offered it. There was plenty of ice cream in the freezer if she had a sweet-tooth attack later. Kayla always made sure they were stocked up on it, but she ran every morning to counter the effects of her guilty pleasure. It was amazing that Kristen was able to stay in such good shape because unlike her sisters, she didn't work out. Chasing children all day was all the workout she needed.

Randy walked her to her car. He gave her brief kiss good night, and she could swear she felt the earth shift to the left then right itself. She missed his touch more than she thought. When she was able to open her eyes again, she released him and watched him walk to his truck. She climbed into her own vehicle, and they headed in separate directions toward their own houses. During the drive home, she wondered how long the laughter between her and Randy would last. After the events leading to the end of their relationship last time, she knew anything could happen. Deep down she hoped the happiness would last forever.

* * * *

"Where are we going, Randy?"

He smiled as he waited for her to lock the front door. "If I told you, then it wouldn't be a surprise, would it?"

She shook her head, and he led her to his truck. After a short drive, they stopped at the park. She looked over at him in surprise. It was one of her favorite places. Being here reminded her of fond childhood memories, of her mother and grandparents push her on the swings. Randy opened her door and helped her out before reaching behind her seat. He pulled out a blanket and picnic basket. After finding a shady spot, he took out two ham sandwiches with all the fixings, potato chips, and dill pickle slices. They ate in silence and enjoyed the cool breeze while watching the kids come through with their parents. They greeted everyone they knew, and she enjoyed watching the children play. She struggled to clear images of watching her own children play.

A feeling sadness came over her when she thought about it. If she and Randy had stayed together, they would be married and have kids. She looked over at Randy, who was watching the other kids play and knew without a doubt they would. She closed her eyes and tamped down the anger threatening to bubble up to the surface. Like Kayla said, she deserved to be angry and upset, but she couldn't continue to take it out on Randy if she intended to make things work. Besides, Randy was really trying, and it wouldn't be fair to him if she didn't do the same. Still she couldn't hide her disappointment.

When they finished their lunch, Randy packed up all of the remains from the picnic and put them back in the basket. She watched as he sat the basket aside prior to standing.

"Let's go for a walk."

She gave him a surprised look but took the hand he extended and allowed him to pull her to her feet. He led her through the park. "I didn't notice it when we were younger, but this is a beautiful park."

She looked up at him and smiled. "Yes, it is. I haven't been here in a while, but it is still pretty."

"Well you can thank the seniors. They have put a lot of effort into cleaning up the community for their class project."

Kristen nodded. "I heard Kayla mentioning something about it."

"I'm glad because Wade likes it here. If I can't bring him, my mom tries to." Randy grinned. "How is teaching at the high school going for Kayla?"

"It is going pretty well. Kayla says it's almost like being back in high school at times."

Randy smiled. "Well then, she must hate that."

She laughed. "Believe it or not, we had fun in high school. Mostly due to the fact I had two sisters to share it with. I'm also glad that I was able to share it with you."

He paused, looking deep into her eyes. There was an emotion there she couldn't decipher. "It was a good time for me, too. One thing I wonder about now is if you will love me anywhere near the amount you used to during that time."

She was speechless, but it was a good thing because she couldn't admit to him that it was something he would never have to worry about. She had never stopped loving him.

When he stopped, she looked over at him. "Let's sit down for a moment."

She nodded and sat down on the bench next to him. He stared out at the playground, and she took the chance to study him.

"Kristen, did you ever think about having a family with me?"

She gave him a stunned look. "Of course, I did. I thought about getting married as well."

"Do you still think about it?"

She shook her head. "That isn't a fair question, Randy."

He smiled. "You might be right. However, I will admit that I do."

She remained silent. What was she supposed to say? Randy reached out and took her hand in his giving it a tight squeeze.

"I know that I will never be able to say sorry enough." He sighed. "I know that you may not believe me, but I can understand the hurt that you are going through, and it was never my intention."

She made a small sound of frustration before pulling her hand from his. "How can you say you understand, Randy? You have no idea what it is like to have the person you love walk away with know explanation. So, *tell me,* Randy, how do you *know* how I feel?"

"Because Lila did it to me," he responded softly.

Even through her anger, she heard his words, but she didn't understand them. She looked over at him and found him hunched forward with his elbows resting on his knees.

"What did you say?"

"I said that Lila left me."

She was at a loss for words. What was he saying? What did he mean by the statement? Closing her eyes she knew she wouldn't find out until she asked. "Tell me what happened, Randy?"

Randy glanced up at her briefly, and the pain she saw there was staggering. She reached out and laid a gentle hand on his shoulder. "Tell me what happened, Randy. I would like to know. I'm not sure we can go forward until I do."

She felt a twinge of guilt for pushing him, but it was true. She did need to know. Maybe it would provide her with the knowledge she needed to move forward.

"Lila and I met when she came to Baxley to stay with her aunt and uncle. We bumped into each other at the store because neither of us was paying attention. We hit it off instantly, and soon we were dating."

He paused sighing deeply. "Lila told me everything that I needed to hear, and I believed her. It turns out they were empty words. Lila became pregnant, and she panicked. I thought that it was because she didn't think I would marry her, but I assured her that I would."

His laugh was devoid of humor. "Even though I didn't love her, I cared about her, and I thought we could at least try to give our child a normal home. She seemed to calm down when I bought the ring, and everything was okay for a while."

He smiled. "Then she had Wade, and to me, nothing could be more perfect. The first time I held him was indescribable. I made the vow then to be the best husband and father that I could be no matter what it took."

He paused again rubbing his hand across his eyes. "Then Lila left. She took Wade over to my mom's house and said she was going to the store, but she never came back. When my mom called me, I almost went crazy thinking something happened to her. I called her aunt and uncle, and they hadn't heard from her. I didn't know what to think."

He looked over at her, and the pain there almost blinded her. "When I got home, there was a note on the table from Lila telling me that she couldn't stay with me and Wade. We weren't the life that she wanted."

Kristen couldn't hold back the gasp that escaped her. She felt a sharp pain in her chest as she reached out to Randy. She was at a loss for words. Never would she have imagined Randy had gone through what he had.

"I'm sorry that you went through something so horrible, Randy."

He shook his head as he looked at her. "Don't be. In a lot of ways, I have come to realize it was my punishment for what I did to you."

Her eyes widened in horror. "*Oh my God,* you *can't* think that?"

He gave her a look that told her he did. She shook her head and knew that she could reason with him. She could only tell him how she felt. He had been honest with her. Now it was her turn to do the same.

"What about Wade? Is he a part of your punishment?"

Randy gave her a shocked look. "No. He is the best thing that came from my relationship with Lila."

She sighed. Both she and Randy had suffered through heartache. It was complete irony that it was another connection they shared. Still they had a lot to work through.

"I don't know Lila myself, but from what you say she sounds like an awful and selfish person. Trust me, in the end, it was her loss."

He gave her a small smile. "So you see I do understand heartache."

She shook her head. "It doesn't even compare. I just wish you had trusted me."

He reached for her hands. "I did trust you, Kristen. What can I say to make you believe it was me?"

She paused. "That's the problem. I do believe that it was you, and that is what scares me."

He gave her a confused look. "Why?"

"Because I wonder what your reaction will be the next time you doubt yourself."

* * * *

Randy exhaled softly as not to disturb Kristen. After his revealing conversation with her, he convinced her to rejoin him on the blanket. Now they were lying together with her in his arms. It was something that he didn't realize how much he missed until he had her there.

She still fit against him perfectly. It reminded him of the first time they had spent the night with each other. He had gone up to Athens for the weekend to visit her. It had been a wonderful weekend one that ended with her walking into the living room in the middle of the night and joining him on the futon. When he tried to wake her early the following morning to give her the chance to go back to her room before her sisters started to move about, instead of getting up to leave, she chose to snuggle closer to him and told him she was an adult and capable of making her own decisions. He took in her determined expression then retook his position beside her and pulling her back into his embrace. When he woke up the next time, Kristen was sprawled over him, and Kayla had been in the kitchen cooking breakfast. Kristen must have smelled the breakfast because she had begun to stir from her sleep.

When her sleepy brown eyes had opened, he had placed a brief kiss on her lips in a greeting. When he pulled back she had smiled greeting him back. In that moment he had known he wanted a future with Kristen.

There were several fond memories he had with Kristen. Another was the time he had driven in from school to take Kristen out for her eighteenth birthday. He had shown up with a formal invitation asking for her to accompany him for the evening. She had been excited yet shy and unsure about the invite. It had taken him ten minutes to convince her he was serious about his invite. Once she had agreed he gave her the final details, and everything had been set. Yet, he hadn't been prepared for the Kristen who had stood in front him on the porch that night. It had been the first time he had seen her with her hair down. It wasn't as long now, but it was still spectacular. It had been the first time he realized she was a woman. They had gone out and had a wonderful time. From that point, they had become almost inseparable. He looked down when he heard Kristen exhale softly. She was relaxed and accepting of his embrace, something a few weeks ago he would have never imagined. Now he just had to figure out what to do to keep her there.

* * * *

Kristen stiffened her spine when someone whistled at her. She knew who it was before she straightened. There was just one person she knew who could whistle in such an irritating fashion. She turned to look into Randy's grinning face. She had the pleasure of watching his smile disappear when he saw the look on her face. He walked into the small room she called her office and closed the door behind him. Her eyebrows rose when he locked it, but she remained silent.

"Tough day?"

She groaned. "That would be putting it lightly. Zebbie called in sick. Also, I have never seen so many sick children in my life. Sean has a stomach virus, and he has thrown up more times than I can count. Felix seems to have the urge to use the bathroom and often, but he wasn't making it to the restroom at least not on time."

She paused for a breath. "Troy has a runny nose and wants to touch everything and everyone after he uses his hand for a Kleenex, and that's just the tip of the iceberg."

Before she could continue, he placed a finger over her lips. "Take a deep breath and relax."

Kristen closed her eyes and exhaled a soft breath of relief. Thank goodness it was lunchtime and Troy and Sean had been picked up. The last thing she could afford was a day care of sick children. All of Felix's clothes had been washed, and he wore a new set. She crossed her fingers hoping they would stay dry. At least things couldn't get any worse. Until school let out, there were five kids left in the day care, more than manageable for her and Gerri, who was serving the children their lunch.

Gerri had told instructed her to go to the office and take a break because it was obvious she needed one.

She opened her eyes when Randy stepped closer to her.

"Now," he said while he took off his hat and sat it on the desk. "If you don't mind, I would like to greet you properly."

She wasn't able to respond because he had already brought his lips down on top of hers. The kiss was soft, long, and passionate. When he lifted his mouth from hers, they were both breathing hard. She smiled as she looked into his sexy eyes. "Thank you. You just made my day better."

His gave her a wicked grin that sent shivers down her spine. From experience, she knew the seductive expression meant trouble.

"I want to give you something else that will last you for the rest of the day."

She gave him a wary look, and he laughed. Reaching around her, he moved a stack of papers out of harm's way then lifting her onto the desk. She gasped at his action.

"Randy, what are you doing?"

He didn't respond because he was too busy sliding his hand under her long, flowing skirt. She went to grab his hands, but he was elusive. "What are you doing?"

He stopped and looked into her eyes. "Do you trust me?"

She nodded without hesitation. His eyes told her he planned to make good on his promise. "Then lift your hips for me."

She lifted her hips, and he slid off her underwear. She gasped in shock, and he whispered, "Thank you."

What was she thinking? They were in her day care, and even though the children were on the other side of the building this entire situation could be a disaster.

Her mouth fell open to scold him, but his mouth found hers and cut off her response. She melted in his arms, moaning when his mouth slid from hers and down to her throat. He began to unbutton her blouse, placing kisses upon her chest. She protested when he skipped over her breast. They were aching for his touch. "Randy—"

"Shh."

"But—"

She bit her lip trying to fight a moan, and he smiled.

"Someone could pass by and hear you." She gave him the evil eye when he said what she had been try to.

Still it quieted her, and she dropped her head back as Randy's kisses made her forget where she was. They always had. She rested her forehead against his shoulder in surrender. It had been a long time since she felt his touch, and she wanted it

"Please tell me you locked the door."

"Yes, I did."

She exhaled deeply. "Did anyone see you come in?"

"Yes and no."

She gave him a puzzled look. "What do you mean?"

"I just dropped Wade off so Zebbie saw me, and when she went to take him to his classroom, I snuck back here to you."

Kristen shook her head. "I am glad it was you, but that is why I have the security camera on the front entrance."

He smiled. "Very smart thinking."

She nodded. "I thought so, too. How was Wade's dentist appointment?"

Randy chuckled while he pulled her to the edge of the desk. "Excellent. All of his teeth are in perfect condition. Now back to helping you relax."

He sank to his knees, and her eyes widened. "Randy, what are you doing?"

He avoided answering the question. "Open your legs."

She stiffened at his blunt command. It was due more to the fact she hadn't been intimate with anyone in a long time. Six years to be exact.

"Excuse me?"

He looked up at her and chuckled. "Could you open your legs, please?"

Kristen knew she should keep her legs closed. She knew what would happen, but she wanted this. She needed his touch. Wanted to know if it was still familiar. Closing her eyes, she opened her legs.

"Brace yourself."

His mouth touched the sensitive opening between her thighs, and she gasped. Her breath caught in her throat, and she stiffened. He lifted his head.

"You are supposed to relax."

"Easy for you to say," she whispered.

How could she relax when he was driving her insane with need? Instead of responding, he lowered his head again, and she lost all capability of thinking. The man was good at everything he did. At least he seemed to be. He seemed to be making her hotter while smothering out the flame at the same time. She didn't realize she was encouraging him until she looked down and saw her hands in his hair. A groan of displeasure slipped from between her lips, and he pulled away, but he made his way back up her body until he was standing.

His mouth covered hers while he placed his fingers where his mouth had been, and she gasped. His mouth muffled the sound, and he continued to drive her mindless with pleasure. A smooth glide of his tongue left her tasting her own exotic flavor.

He drove her higher with pleasure until she arched into his touch and let out a cry of fulfillment that he muffled by his mouth. The powerful orgasm left her drained but relaxed. Randy had kept his promise. He pulled her close, and she melted into his embrace enjoying the afterglow of her release. Several heartbeats later, he pulled back and helped her straighten her clothes. She tried to ignore the conceited expression on his face.

"Now you should be relaxed for the rest of the day."

Kristen chuckled in amusement and gave him a drowsy but satisfied look. She wanted to hit him for being so smug but couldn't muster the energy, especially when he was right.

"That is going to help me out for the rest of the week."

Randy tipped his hat to her. "Glad to be of service to you."

Wrapping his arms around her waist, he lifted her off the desk and sat her on her own two feet. He made sure she was steady before moving back. Placing a brief kiss on her lips, he reached for his hat and set it on his head. "Can I give you a call later on this evening?"

She gave him a look of surprise. "You have to ask? I would be offended if you didn't."

"Good. Well, I have to get going, but I will talk to you later."

She nodded and watched him unlock the door and peek out. She assumed the coast was clear when he opened it wider and stepped out. She followed him and closed the door behind them. "Let's go this way."

She led him through a side door and back around to the front of the building where his truck was waiting. He reached for his keys, and she ran her hand over the side of his truck. "You know I would like to take a ride in this with you sometime."

He looked at her in surprise, and she knew her veiled statement had been understood. "Well, I will have to see what I can do."

Chapter Seven

"*He did what?*" Keirra exclaimed.

Kayla giggled. "It is about time."

Keirra elbowed her. "You aren't helping."

Kristen shook her head. This was why she was hesitant to tell her sisters personal business sometimes. She was telling them about the events that had occurred today but left out the details. Yet, her sisters had enough of an imagination to figure out the rest on their own, and they hadn't disappointed. So far it seemed she had had the most exciting day.

Kayla waved her hand in dismissal to Keirra. "Don't mind this one over here. If I had a guy who was an identical twin to Matthew McConaughey, I would be doing the same exact thing you are."

Kristen snapped her fingers in realization. She smiled at her sisters. "That's who he reminds me of."

"Who Matthew McConaughey or Randy?"

Keirra stuck her tongue out at Kayla, and Kristen cleared her throat before they could get started. "So what do you guys think I should do?"

"I say you don't do anything. He is a cop. You are walking into dangerous territory."

Kayla groaned. "Keirra, lay off of the cop thing already."

Turning her attention to Kristen, Kayla placed her arm around her younger sister.

"This is a decision you have to make. It is an important decision because once it's made you can't get it back."

"Do you think I should tell him?"

"I wouldn't. Twenty-eight-year-old virgins tend to scare men off. Trust me,

I know," Keirra scoffed.

Kayla chuckled. "And all this time I thought it was your attitude."

Kristen put her hands up and waved them around frantically trying to distract the two of them before they could get carried away. It got her sisters' attention like she had intended for it to. "Cut it out, you two."

They both gave her a sheepish look and apologized. Keirra responded in a soft voice. "This is your decision to make. Just keep in mind it is one you have to live with."

Kristen groaned and leaned her head back against the couch. It was true she was a twenty-eight-year-old virgin, but then again, so were her sisters. They had made a pact to each other to wait until they found a man they each thought was worthy. She always thought Randy to be worthy, but things had never gone far. Several of their make out sessions had been hot and heavy, but it had never gone beyond that. Somehow, he had always known how far to go. When he called tonight, it would be a subject she would bring up.

She stood and stretched. "Keirra, the dinner was excellent tonight. Thank you."

Keirra smiled. "Don't forget it's your turn tomorrow."

Keirra laughed. Dinner duty wasn't a favorite of anyone except Kayla, but they all rotated to keep it fair. "I know. I have already taken out the meat to defrost."

Kayla smacked her lips in anticipation. "I am looking forward to it."

"I am going to go upstairs and take my shower, but I'll be back down in a little while."

Her sisters nodded. "Okay."

She made her way upstairs. She took a quick shower and, fifteen minutes, later returned downstairs. When she made her way into the kitchen, she saw her sisters had already started on the dishes. Walking over to the sink, she joined in, and they had the kitchen cleaned up in no time.

Kayla yawned. "I guess I'm more tired than I thought I was." She stretched. "I am going to head to bed. Don't stay up too late."

Keirra was already heading for the stairs herself. "Don't worry. I won't."

Not seeing any reason to stay downstairs by herself, Kristen trailed her sisters up the stairs. They all murmured good nights to each other then proceeded to their rooms. Kristen crawled into her bed and turned on the bedside lamp. She lay down and then picked up the picture frame containing the last family photo they had taken together. She smiled at how happy everyone looked.

She put the picture down and then picked up another that showed Keirra, Kayla and herself just a year ago. The picture depicted happiness, but it was strange not to have her mother and father in it. She missed her parents so much, and it was times like these when she was glad she had two sisters.

Closing her eyes, she wondered what life would have been like if their father had lived. Would she have gotten the chance to know Randy like she did? A smile came to her face when her cell phone rang. Picking it up, she saw Randy's number and answered.

"Hello."

"Hey yourself. How was the rest of your day?"

She closed her eyes and tried to push aside the memories of their erotic encounter. "It was okay. The kids were calm the rest of the day. I also did my best to make sure all of the kids who looked like they might be coming down with something were quarantined, but I would still keep an eye on Wade and give him an extra dose of vitamins if you have them."

"Thanks for the warning."

Kristen hoped he wouldn't get sick. She hoped that none of the other kids became sick. Another day like today would be too much.

"So your dose of medicine held you over for the day?"

She laughed at his analogy. The fact she had sneaked him out of the day care center after an illicit tryst made her feel like a teenager again. She paused before responding. "Yes, it did, and speaking of which, have you ever thought about us making love?"

He was silent, and for a moment she thought he hadn't heard her. She opened her mouth to tell him to ignore the question, but he responded. "Yes, I have. Have you?"

"Yes."

She closed her eyes and shook her head. She did feel like a teenager now, one discussing a taboo subject. "What made you ask?"

"Well, after today, I just wondered if you had thought about it."

Randy chuckled. "If I recall, you once accused me of thinking about sex all the time."

"Well, I think it might have been true at that point." Kristen thought back to some of their make out sessions but couldn't remember a time when the statement rang true. He had never let it go past kissing and touching over her clothes and sometimes underneath in a fashion very similar to what he had done today. But he had never tried to test the limits and would always stop if she asked him to.

"You could be right, but I always respected you for sticking to your values."

"What do you mean?"

He chuckled. "You told me you were going to wait until you were certain you wanted to make love, and I respected your decision."

She cleared her throat. "So it wouldn't surprise you to find out that I am still a virgin?" He paused, and she knew he was shocked by her confession. "There has been no one else since you, but I know you are the one."

She heard him drop the phone and curse. He picked the phone up again and dropped it once more. She laughed and heard him fumble to gain control of the phone.

"Do you mind repeating what you just said?"

She spoke slowly so she was sure he understood her. "I said you are the one."

When he remained silent, she became nervous wondering what he thought about her confession—the importance of it. She tried to lighten the mood by teasing him a little. "Did you drop the phone again?"

* * * *

No, he hadn't dropped the phone again, but he was shocked. The fact she considered him to be good enough to be her first humbled him. He hadn't been Lila's first, but she had been his, and now he hated that she had been. Nothing more would be more meaningful to him than to be Kristen's first. In several ways, he always thought she would be. On the other hand, he was no longer awkward like he had been in the beginning with Lila, and he knew he would be able to please Kristen. Then again, he always had. Still, he was hesitant because he knew how significant this was for her—for both of them. He cleared his throat before speaking. "Are you sure about this?"

"Yes, I am very certain."

He heard the conviction in her voice, and he smiled. When Kristen made a decision, it meant she had thought it through. "Okay then, but we are still going to take this slow."

He heard Kristen snap her fingers. "Darn, and here I was thinking I could come over tonight and slip between the sheets with you."

He laughed. "You have been spending too much time with Keirra."

Kristen laughed in response, but they both knew it was a true statement. He knew firsthand how close Kristen and her sisters were. They were inseparable, and because of that, there were times when her sisters did rub off on her, and there were times when she rubbed off on them. The good thing was it didn't occur often. Otherwise, there would be more trouble than there normally was. Kristen had always been special to him, and he had to be to her considering what she just revealed to him. It was hard to contain himself because it was the one thing he had yet to share with her. It was also the one he couldn't wait to share with her.

Randy began formulating a plan in his mind. He wanted to be prepared to make it special for her when the time arose. "What do you say we get together for dinner at my place this weekend and we take it from there?"

"That sounds good to me. Do you need me to bring anything?"

"No. All you have to do is bring yourself. I will take care of everything else."

She sighed, and he could understand her slight hesitance. What she was getting ready to agree to could make a person nervous. He just hoped she wasn't going to change her mind. Still, the last thing he wanted to do was pressure Kristen into any unfair situation.

He had always felt she wasn't experiencing the life she should be because of her serious relationship with him. Yet, this was one thing he did want to experience with her and would go to any lengths to make sure it was an experience she would never forget.

"Okay," she whispered.

He held back his sigh of relief. "I will give you a call and let you know what time Saturday."

"Okay."

He fought a yawn but was unsuccessful. It had been a long day.

"Did you have a hard day?"

He smiled at her question. "Yes and no. I have finished conducting the interviews for the vacant deputy position and thought I would have a decision made by now, but I don't. We are all having to pick up extra patrols right now."

"Do you have anyone in mind?"

He had three of the five candidates he interviewed in mind but just one he considered making a job offer to.

"Yes I do. I need to do a few more reference checks. I will make my decision after they are complete."

"Well, good luck. I'm sure you will find a great replacement."

"I'm sure I will, too. I don't want to keep you much longer. I just wanted to give you a call to see how the rest of your day went."

"Well, thank you for keeping your word. It means a lot."

He grinned. "You know I always do, but you have a good day tomorrow, and if I don't see you, just know I will be thinking about you."

"I will be thinking about you too, Randy," she whispered. "Good night."

"Sweet dreams."

Randy hung up the phone and rolled onto his back. He looked up at the ceiling. Soon, he was asleep and having very sweet dreams about Kristen.

* * * *

Kristen wiped her mouth and leaned back in her chair. She was stuffed and everything had been delicious. "You are a much better cook than I remember."

Randy smiled. "Thank you. I had to learn a lot over the past few years. Wade is my toughest critic."

She shook her head and smiled at the mention of Wade. He was an adorable kid, and she had grown fond of him. She told Randy that it would be okay for Wade to join them for dinner, but Randy had insisted his parents watch Wade. When she knocked on Randy's door and entered his house earlier, she knew it had been a good idea for Wade not to be there. She might not be experienced, but she knew seduction when she saw it. Candles were lit all over the entire house. She had followed him through his living room and into the kitchen where the set up had been the same.

He held out her chair while she sat and poured her a glass of wine before walking over to the oven and removing two plates he had warming in the oven. Randy set one in front of her and the other across from her. Once he had taken his seat, he toasted to a great evening to come and they began to eat. They made small talk during the meal. She noticed he still had the ability to make her laugh a lot. He told her about his brother and two sisters she hadn't seen in years. Randy was the oldest, Emily followed him, Cody followed her, and Blair was the baby of the family. From what he said, the Stroud family seemed to be doing okay.

So was she after the wonderful meal Randy fed her. He stood and began to clean up. She stood to help him, and he protested but she wanted to help. It would give her something to do with her hands. This was the first time she had seen Randy outside of his uniform since she came face-to-face with him at the day care. The man was so sexy he made her eyes hurt. There was also his air-dried hair that looked like the wind had touched it a few times today. Combined with his facial hair, he had a tousled Matthew McConaughey look, and it made it very difficult for her to keep her hands to herself. Randy rinsed the last of the dishes, and she dried it and set it in the dish rack.

He turned to face her. "Let's go into the living room."

She nodded, and he led the way. He turned on the television, and they both went around the living room blowing out the candles. When the last one was blown out, they met at the couch. He picked up the remote.

"Any special request?"

She shook her head and laughed when he changed the channel and a popular cartoon came on the screen. "You still have your obsession with cartoons I see."

"Wade is starting to obsess with me. It also helps that I have him around because I can get away with blaming it on him most of the time."

She shook her head and settled in next to him laughing at a few of the scenes. Randy put his arms around her and pulled her close.

"You seem to have a good memory," he whispered in her ear.

"I always did when it came to you."

She grinned and watched the screen but didn't pay attention to what was on it. Her mind was on the man she was sitting next to. Randy had done well for himself, and she wondered if he knew. It was obvious Lila's actions affected his self-esteem. The man next to her had lost some of the confidence he had had when they were younger. She could see the hesitance in his eyes on occasion, hear it in his voice when he spoke. It worried her because she knew it could affect their relationship. She shifted closer to him whispering his name. When he looked down at her, she gave him a small smile. He studied her, and she saw a look of concern fall upon his face.

"Is something wrong?"

"Yes and no. I guess I just have a lot on my mind."

He turned off the television. "Do you want to talk about it?"

She studied him for a momentarily before responding. "I'm afraid you will hurt me again."

He gave her a puzzled look. "Why would you think I'd want to hurt you?"

She shook her head. "I know you wouldn't hurt me on purpose, but it is obvious that you are still affected by what Lila did to you."

She reached out and touched his face. "Your eyes are different. When you speak to me it's different than it used to be. I hear a hesitance that didn't used to be there."

He nodded. "I am different, and so are you, Kristen. You are more confident, more outspoken. They are changes that I like because they add to who you are." He sighed. "I'm not sure what you want me to say."

Kristen closed her eyes. "I want you to tell me that you are over what Lila did to you."

He remained silent, and her heart lurched with pain. She thought she would be prepared for this, but she wasn't.

"Look at me, Kristen."

At the pleading note in his voice, she opened her eyes. The sadness she saw in them hurt her.

"I'm not sure I can get over what Lila did to me." The corner of his mouth tilted up. "It would be like me asking you to get over me breaking up with you."

She gave him a heated look. "It's not the same."

He nodded. "It is the same, but I would never ask you that because I'm not sure that anyone can get over the pain of getting hurt. I think that one learns to live with the pain, and hopefully, they forgive the person who inflicted it at some point."

She remained silent. He had a good point, and she hated it. She wasn't over the pain that she and her family had been caused by the man that shot and killed her father, but in time the pain became less, and she had forgiven the shooter.

Randy brought her hand up to his lips and placed a kiss on it. "So I would love to tell you that I am over Lila but not for the reasons you think. I no longer have feelings for Lila, but Wade does. He still has a hurt that I can't fix. Every time I have to explain to Wade why Lila left, it is like reopening the wound."

Kristen paused. She never thought about it in that way. She should have because she shared a similar experience herself. After he father had been shot in the line of duty, she constantly questioned why it had to be her dad and not someone else's. It had been the same when her mother passed away. She had an advantage over Wade. At her age she had been able to understand a lot more.

She looked at the man in front her and felt admiration for him.

"Wade is lucky to have you."

Randy shook his head. "I am fortunate to have Wade."

He grinned at her. "I'm also lucky that you are giving me a chance to prove to you that I do care for you and want you back in my life."

She leaned closer to him. "By me giving you a chance, do you think we can make it this time around?"

He smiled before bringing his hand up to cup her face. "If we work together, I don't see why we can't."

She watched Randy lean toward her. When his lips touched hers, she sighed. He pulled her closer, and she ended up on his lap. She brought her arms up and encircled his neck. She hardly noticed when he broke off the kiss to take off her shirt.

He pulled back and studied her. "Are you sure about this because I don't want you to have any regrets?"

She sighed with contentedness. This was a moment that she used to dream about. She didn't want to back out now. "Yes."

Randy leaned closer to her. "Wrap your arms around my neck."

She did what he asked, and he wrapped his arms around her. He stood with her and headed for the stairs. She had no idea how he saw where he was going but then again it was his house. Encircling her legs around his narrow waist she laid her head on his shoulder and held on. He went up the stairs and entered the first room on the right. She unwrapped her arms from around his neck when he released her to stand on her own two feet. He undid the button and unzipped the zipper of her skirt. It slid over her hips and to the floor with a whisper. She brought her hands up to his waist and found his belt buckle. Their eyes met while she undid the belt and tugged his shirt out of his khaki pants. She lifted his shirt, and before it hit the ground, she'd settled her hands on his chest. The contact was brief because he began to strip the both of them.

Within seconds, he had them both of them **undressed** he his breath came out on a pained gasp. "You are more beautiful than I remember."

Kristen blushed. The light coming into the room was coming from the bathroom. She could see his body very well, and the man looked like he had been sculpted from marble. The uniform he wore was very deceptive. His head lowered, and when he found one of her nipples, all ability to think escaped her. She gasped and found herself clutching his hair in her hands. He went to lift his head and her grip tightened until she realized he was only switching to the other. Her legs weakened, and Randy picked her up. He placed her on the bed, and her eyes widened at the sight of his erection.

"You aren't going to fit."

He chuckled while he reached for protection, and she clapped her hand over her mouth. She wanted to die of embarrassment.

"Did I just say that?"

He smiled. "Yes, you did, but don't worry. We are made to fit together."

Her response was forgotten when his hand found the inside of her thighs. She arched into him, moaning when his fingers moved. Within seconds, he had her soaring over the edge. By the time she began to recover, he had donned protection and was sliding into her. His hips thrust forward with need, and she winced again. He bumped up against the barrier, proof she had waited for him. She took a deep breath and tried to relax.

He rested his forehead against hers and looked into her eyes. "Are you okay?"

She nodded, and he sighed. "I don't want to hurt you."

She smiled and brought her hand up to cup his cheek. "You won't."

He stared at her, and she felt brief panic. She didn't want him to change his mind. "I'm sure about this, Randy."

She sighed in relief when he covered her mouth with his in a gentle kiss while he reached down and captured her hips between his hands. She leaned into his kiss, and he thrust deep into her breaking through the barrier of virginity.

Kristen stiffened beneath him, and he captured her cry of pain. She pulled her mouth away from his, but he held her close. He whispered soothing words to her, and she began relax. He brushed her hair out of the way, and his face came into view. His concerned expression touched her, and she relaxed more.

"Are you okay?"

She took a deep, slow, and shaky breath. "I think so."

"Am I still hurting you?"

She shook her head. He wasn't hurting her like he had earlier. The pain was subsiding and being replaced with something else. Looking up, she glanced at his face. She saw true concern. Taking a deep breath, Kristen realized the pain was almost non-existent. She exhaled softly. "I'm okay."

He pulled back and then slid back inside of her. Her breath caught in her throat at the pleasure that now replaced the sensation of pain. With a few more thrusts she brought her hands up and grabbed his shoulders.

"Better?"

She nodded, not having the ability to speak. Her stomach and thighs tightened giving him the first signs of her impending orgasm. He slid his hand down in between them, and when his fingers found her heated core, she let her head fall back, and she cried out.

"Come for me," he whispered, and she did.

Her body tightened around him pulled him into his own unexpected orgasm. Several deep breaths later, he withdrew from her and, pulling her with him, rolled onto his side. He placed a kiss against her forehead, and she sighed.

"Thank you."

He looked down at her. "For?"

She smiled. "Making this a wonderful experience."

His arms tightened around her. Kristen snuggled closer.

"Please tell me you are going to stay the night. Now that I have you in my arms I want you here for the entire night."

Her insides melted at his sincere words. He moved away from her, getting out of bed. He headed into his bathroom, and when he returned he was carrying a towel. She watched him as he came to the bed. He sat on the edge and smiled at her.

"Roll over onto your back."

She followed his request. "Close your eyes."

His hands opened her to him. She fought to stay relaxed at the intimate position he had put her in, but it wasn't anymore intimate than what they'd already shared. He used the cool towel to wipe away the evidence of the passion they had just shared and soothe away some of the ache she felt.

When he was done, she opened her eyes and saw him toss the towel aside. He stood, reached for the covers, and pulled them up before joining Kristen in his bed. He pulled her into his arms, and she went willingly. She loved being where she always felt she belonged.

Chapter Eight

Kristen's eyes snapped open when she realized she wasn't in her own bed. She looked around the room and realized last night hadn't been a dream. Her gaze went to the doorway when Randy entered it. He carried a tray of food in his hands.

"Good morning, Sleeping Beauty."

"Good morning." She hid a yawn behind her hand. "What time is it?"

"A few minutes after eleven."

Wrapping his bedspread around her, she sat up amazed she slept so late. She gasped at the delicious ache between her thighs. He set the tray on her lap, and she inhaled its aroma with appreciation.

The tray he sat in front of her contained two plates. One held several pieces of toast, bacon, and eggs. The other held slices of honeydew melon, grapes, and strawberries. There was a cup of coffee for him and cup of milk for her. She looked up in surprise. He remembered everything she liked. These were things she could eat all day long. She was also crazy about milk and drank it with every meal if she had the chance, although food wasn't a necessity to accompany it.

He joined her on the bed, careful not to bump the tray. "Did you sleep well?"

She nodded He reached for the remote and turned on the television. Tom and Jerry ran across the screen, and she laughed. He picked up a piece of honeydew melon and offered it to her.

Taking the bite he offered, chewing it slowly while he took a bite himself. They repeated the process until the food had been finished off. He sat the tray aside, and she yawned. Randy opened his arms, and she snuggled closer to him. It wasn't long before she was asleep with the soft rumble of his laughter in her ear.

* * * *

"Randy, I am a little sore."

He frowned. "Are you sure I wasn't too rough with you?"

She looked down at the man she had just gotten out of the shower with. After the walk in the park, they realized a cool shower would be refreshing. It had been, but now he knelt down in front her, toweling her dry. He definitely seemed to be getting sidetracked with the distraction in front of him.

"I'm sure."

"Okay, but I think this is the opportune time for me to show you the wonders of foreplay."

She laughed. "I think I have unleashed a beast."

He chuckled as he straightened. "I think you may be right."

After lifting her in his arms, he carried her to the bed, and she wrapped her arms and legs around him.

"You know this doesn't change anything, right? We still have a few things to work out."

He shrugged. "Then we will talk, but later."

Her eyebrows lifted at his lack of concern. Yet, the things he was doing with the towel made it hard to think.

She tried to speak, and he quieted her. "Shh. We can talk more after I finish drying you off."

Before she could say anything, he came up over her and cupped her breasts. His thumbs turned her nipples into hard peaks. She wanted to tell him what he was doing had nothing to do with drying her off. It was having the exact opposite effect, but she swallowed her words when he leaned forward and took one nipple into his mouth, then the other. She moaned and writhed against him. She ran her fingers through his hair and tried to pull him up for a kiss. The man had a talented mouth. He slid lower, his lips leaving a trail of desire as he went. His hands came up and parted her thighs. He continued to trail kisses along the inside of her thigh making sure he didn't touch the part of her aching the most. A growl of frustration escaped Kristen, and it ended with a cry when his lips found her softness. She arched toward him in response to his sensuous foreplay. She moaned when his fingers joined his mouth. He was making her burn, and the fire was getting hotter.

She cried out and clutched the bedspread when her orgasm snuck up on her an erupted inside her. He came back up beside her, and fighting to catch her breath, she reached for him in the process. He caught her hands.

"If you don't want to be anymore sore than you are now, you might want to leave that alone."

She gave him a look full of need. "I need you inside me."

He let go of her hand, and she found his erection. She sighed in relief when he reached for a condom before coming up over her. He lifted her legs around his waist and slid deep into her. She shifted against him needing more of him. He placed his hand under her bottom and lifted her to him. He stilled when she gasped.

"Am I hurting you?"

Yes, he was, but it was a good hurt, the kind she welcomed. She shook her head, and he lifted her hips. He groaned and began to thrust into her, setting up a rhythm she struggled to keep up with. He was overwhelming her from every imaginable angle. Leaning down he kissed her, and she tasted herself on his lips. She almost screamed when he stopped moving only to have him unwrap her legs from around his waist and place them over his arms. She did scream when he thrust back into her, and she screamed again when she climaxed. Her body clamped down on his pulling him over the edge with her. He released his own shout, her name being on the end of it. When he fell forward, he rolled to the side, taking care not to crush her with his weight, and she fought to control her breathing.

"We shouldn't have done this," she complained.

He looked down at her. "Why not?"

She sighed. "Because, now I don't want to leave let alone move."

His expression told her he had no intention of rushing her off at all. "You don't have to."

"Yes, I do. I need to get home and straighten up a few things plus get ready for tomorrow."

They lay there for a little while longer, neither of them wanting to leave. She scooted closer to him, and his embrace tightened, and she understood why. She knew it might be a while before he could do so again with the hectic week that was coming up. She looked over at him when he sat up.

"Okay, it's getting late, and if we don't get up now, we won't. Besides, I'm going over to my parents' for dinner and to pick up Wade."

Her eyebrows furrowed. "Are you sure your parents didn't mind watching him this long?"

"They have watched him longer in the past."

She sat up when he got out of bed and pulled on a pair of pants. Sighing softly, she climbed out of bed. She wasn't ready for this to be over. He handed her clothes to her. She hoped no one would notice she was still wearing the skirt and blouse she had worn over to his place. The items had been washed thanks to Randy, but Baxley was still small enough for the rumor mill to reach everyone. Once she was dressed, she looked at Randy and saw he was waiting on her.

"Are you ready?"

"Yes."

He took her hand and led the way downstairs. He paused to let her pick up her purse when they passed through the living room. When he stopped the next time, he pulled her to him and then brought his mouth down on hers. The kiss went on for what seemed like forever, and when he pulled back, she was breathless.

"I hope your kiss will last me all week since it will be this weekend before I get another chance to do it again."

She nodded and had almost forgotten he was going to be finalizing his candidate selection to fill the deputy position. He opened the door and closed it behind him, locking it. They went to her car, and she climbed behind the wheel. After they shared another brief kiss, she started the engine and pulled off. She sighed to herself after she came to the stop sign. Each time, it was getting harder and harder to leave Randy, and she knew a day would come when she didn't want to. She wondered if he would want the same when that time came.

*****

"Are you going to be my mommy?"

Kristen froze. It was the last thing she expected to come out of Wade's mouth. She asked Randy to let him stay home and spend some time with them this weekend because Wade was a large part of Randy's life and she realized they all needed to get along and get to know each other or it wouldn't work. Her relationship with Wade was as vital as the one she was trying to rebuild with Randy. She walked over to the couch and sat down. Kristen motioned for Wade to come and join her. He went straight for her lap, and she let him.

She didn't see anything wrong with building a healthy relationship with Wade. Looking him straight in the eyes, she answered him honestly.

"I'm not sure if I will be or not, but I sure would love to be. You are a wonderful little boy, and I would be lucky to have a son like you."

Wade seemed to be satisfied with the answer, climbed down out of her lap, and wandered out of the room. Seconds later, she heard him talking to Randy. She took the opportunity to stretch out on the couch. She was exhausted from the week. Her eyelids began to droop, and a short time later, she was asleep. When she did awaken, it was to the aroma of dinner. She couldn't make out the smell, but whatever it was smelled delicious. She sat up, got off of the couch, and headed toward the kitchen. She stopped in the doorway smiling at the sight in front of her. Randy stood at the counter preparing a salad. Wade stood in front of a miniature table preparing something himself, but his food and utensils were made of plastic. He was working hard. She could get used to the sight. Her heart skipped a beat at the thought. The last thing she needed to do was give herself false hope. She had to take things slow and not jump to conclusions. She shook her head to clear it before she continued on into the kitchen.

"What are you guys cooking?"

Wade looked up when he heard her voice. He ran to her, and she bent down to scoop him up into her arms. She laughed when she saw the front of his apron.

She read it aloud. "Cutest Little Chef." Randy would be the one to find something so ingenious.

"Did you have a good nap?"

She looked over at Randy and nodded. "Sorry I fell asleep on you guys."

Wade gave her a very solemn look. "It's okay. Daddy said you needed a nap."

Kristen smiled at Wade then she looked over at Randy who had gone back to his food preparation. "Did he?"

Wade's pout made her heart melt. "But I wanted to wake you. I wanted to cook with you."

Kristen felt her smile widen. "Well, next time, I will try to stay awake so we can." She put him down. "What are you guys cooking?"

Wade pointed to the food on his table while he called it out. "Dinner salad, chicken pot pie, and dinner rolls."

She rubbed her hands together in anticipation. "Sounds yummy. Do you need any help?"

Wade shook his head. "No. Dinner is almost ready."

She grinned and looked over at Randy, who was smiling, too. He shook his head before he placed the tomatoes on the salad.

"I have finished everything already and was on my way to wake you." He looked over at Wade. "Clean up your toys so we can get cleaned up for dinner."

Wade began straightening up his mess. Kristen helped him move his miniature table out of the kitchen. Ten minutes later, they were sitting around the table eating. Wade was telling them about his week at the day care, and even though she had experienced it with him she listened to him talk. He seemed to love it, and he was coming out of his stage of shyness.

Over dinner, Wade talked himself out. She knew Randy wanted his son to become more sociable, or at least know how to handle himself in a social situation, another reason Randy told her he decided to put Wade in day care. He also admitted that he had no idea it was her day care until he walked through the front door, but he was glad it had been. She had been touched when he told her that he thought her day care was good for Wade. Kristen beamed as she looked over at Randy.

"So are you happy you chose Eric?"

He nodded, and she knew Eric was the best replacement. He had the experience needed. From what she could tell, he also had the personality. Baxley was a laid-back town, and a Type A personality wouldn't survive in deputy position.

She grinned when she thought about some of the candidates Randy had told her about. He claimed one of the guys he interviewed had left him tempted to perform a drug screen on the spot. Eric on the other hand was easy going, but he was a hard worker, and he was personable.

"He was the right guy for the job."

Kristen reached for her cup. "I agree."

The rest of dinner zipped by quick, and she enjoyed the conversation. Nothing of significance was mentioned. It was just the fact they had a nice conversation. They tried to include Wade in it, and she was delighted by his sense of humor. Still she felt a twinge of pain when she thought about the fact that Wade could be hers. She wanted him to be hers. Yet it was a big risk to be concerned with when things between her and Randy weren't solid

Once they were through eating, the dishes and the kitchen were cleaned.

Randy turned on the television for her. "I am going to take Wade upstairs, give him a bath, and get him ready for bed."

Kristen nodded, and the two of them made their way upstairs. She was still flipping through channels when they returned.

"Have you found anything good yet?"

She shook her head. "No, not yet."

He joined her on the couch, and Wade climbed onto her lap. He was so adorable in his Power Rangers pajamas. She wrapped her arms around him, and he situated himself into her lap where he was comfortable.

"Do you like westerns?"

"Only the ones with Clint Eastwood in them."

He grinned. "Then you are in luck."

She smiled when he switched to the channel showing *The Good, the Bad, and the Ugly*.

They settled in to watch the movie, but he had to get up and put Wade into bed thirty minutes into the movie since he had fallen asleep. Kristen was enjoying holding him, but he had become heavy.

When he returned downstairs, he turned off the television before leading her upstairs to his bedroom. He turned on the television to the movie then stripped down to his underwear. She hoped he didn't expect her to be able to concentrate on the movie with him parading around half naked. But it was obvious he did when he climbed under the covers. Well two could play that game. She went to her overnight bag and pulled out her nightgown. She changed into it and climbed into bed with Randy. He pulled her into his arms, and she settled into them. Wade must have rubbed off on her because she didn't make it through the movie herself. The next time she became aware of her surroundings, it was pitch black and her bladder was crying out to be relieved. Unwrapping herself from around Randy, she got out of bed and headed into the bathroom.

When she came out she crawled back into bed, and Randy pulled her back into his arms and placed a kiss on her forehead.

"I didn't mean to wake you."

He shook his head in dismissal. "I don't mind at all."

"Sorry I fell asleep on you earlier."

He chuckled. "You were tired."

Well she was not the least bit tired now. Kristen leaned back to look at him. Her eyes met his, and he grinned. "What are you thinking about?"

She smiled in return. "I am thinking about kissing you."

She knew by his expression he was going to help her turn her thoughts into reality.

He lowered his head and he kissed her. It was the kind of kiss that made her knees tremble and her heart race. He pulled her close to him and deepened the kiss. She moaned and leaned into him. He pulled back sucking on her bottom lip. Kristen felt it all the way to her toes. His mouth left hers, and he began trailing kisses down her neck.

Another moan escaped her, and his hand slid between their bodies. His lips found hers again while his hand found the wetness between her thighs. She gasped, and he began to build on the desire in her. He took her over the edge quickly. When he reached for her again, she moved away. She wanted to give pleasure to him like he had given her. Giving his shoulders a tentative push, she grinned when he took the hint and rolled onto his back. She came up over him and straddled him like she had seen it done countless times in the movies. He brought his hands to her waist to support her. "What do you plan on doing?"

She shrugged. "Whatever feels good to you."

His eyebrows rose. "Oh? Well then, I am willing to do whatever it is you want to do."

She laughed before leaning forward to place a kiss on his lips. It was her time to experience and explore, and she was going to take her time and enjoy doing so. Her kiss started off light, but when he responded the kiss became passionate. It seemed to go on forever. When she lifted her head they were both breathless. She slid a little lower trailing kisses down his neck like he had done to her, and from his reaction, he enjoyed it. Teasing him, she slid lower, doting attention to his chest. She felt his moan of pleasure more than she heard it, but it let her know what she was doing pleased him. Sliding even lower, she ran her tongue down his washboard stomach. He laughed, and she looked up in surprise. She would have never guessed Randy was ticklish. His erection bumped her chin, and she smiled to herself. She looked down and studied his hard shaft. Unable to help herself, she stuck her tongue out and licked him.

He groaned, and she flicked her tongue out again and then took him into her mouth. Her name came out on a moan. A deep breath later he pulled away from her, and she protested.

"I need to be inside of you."

She wanted him inside of her as well and moved aside when he reached for protection. He covered himself with the condom before pulling her up over him. Her eyes met his, and he brought his hands to her hips again.

"Ride me."

Maneuvering her hips, she lifted until she felt the tip of his erection slide inside of her. She gasped and lowered her hips. It was a different sensation from the very first time. Getting a feel for the new position, she began to move at a slow tempo at first. Leaning forward, she placed a kiss on his lips. Her body began to take over once the passion began to build. Randy's hands came up to guide her hips, and she moaned when he managed to bring them into the right position. Seconds later, she emitted a low and soft scream into his ear, and she experienced her release. He followed close behind her. Her legs began to ache so she moved to the side. She moved next to him. He held her until the inevitable intervened and he had to discard the protection they used. She rolled onto her back and stared at the ceiling. Why was it the more time she spent with Randy the harder it became to remember why she was so hesitant to give him a chance at winning her back?

Chapter Nine

He missed Kristen's warmth when he left the bed. Yet, he had to get rid of the used condom. When he returned she moved into his embrace. He smiled when she snuggled closer to him.

"I hope we didn't disturb Wade."

He looked down at her and grinned. The fact she was always concerned about Wade touched him. There were times when he wished he had Wade with Kristen. He felt like things would be a lot different. Kristen was caring and very attentive toward Wade. There was nothing more he could ask for in a woman than what he found in Kristen. What he liked about her was she wasn't afraid to admit that she didn't know everything. However, she was more than willing to learn the stuff she didn't already know. It was important because to be truthful he was still learning his way himself. After three years there were still things he learned from his son. He was also happy to see the way Wade reacted to having Kristen around. She was the first woman he had become involved with since Wade had been born. It was important that she be able to accept Wade. He didn't doubt that she would because of her love for children, and he had been right.

He placed a kiss on her forehead. "He is a heavy sleeper so there is nothing to worry about."

She yawned, and he smiled. If anyone had told him he would be waking up in the middle of the night making love to a sexy and sensual woman, he wouldn't have believed them. Having Kristen on top of him with her inhibitions put aside had been an experience he couldn't wait to repeat but on another night. He was exhausted, and he wasn't ashamed to admit she had worn him out. He looked down at her and saw her eyes were beginning to drift close. Randy heard her breathing deepen and slow down, and he knew Kristen was sleep. He tightened his arms around her. Moments like these meant a lot to him because he never thought he would have her in his arms again. This weekend was going very well so far.

Closing his own eyes, he went to sleep only to be awakened by the sunlight several hours later. Careful not to disturb Kristen, he climbed out of bed. He grinned when he heard her grumble and reach out for him. A short while later she settled again and was back asleep. He found his underwear next to the bed and her nightgown next to them. He put it where she could find it when she woke up. He went over to his dresser and pulled out a pair of pajama pants then went downstairs. When he entered the kitchen, he put on a pot of coffee and then began rummaging through the kitchen cabinets to see what could be made for breakfast. When the coffee was ready, he poured himself a cup. Looking at the clock, he decided he would let Wade help him choose. His son should be up by now.

After heading back up the stairs, he went to Wade's bedroom. When he didn't see him in the bed, he panicked. He headed for his bedroom, and when he opened the door, Wade was where Randy knew he would be. Wade was tucked up under Kristen's arm and was sound asleep. From the strap sliding off of her shoulder, he realized she had time to prepare. He had been teaching Wade to knock and wait for a response before entering. It must be working. He stood there taking in the picture they made together. Why had he been so stupid to give up Kristen? He shouldn't have assumed that they never had a future together because they never talked about it. Now he had to do whatever it took to get it back to that point. Because even though Kristen was taking the steps to give him another chance it wasn't the same. He could see it when he looked into Kristen's eyes. He turned his gaze back to Kristen, and he watched her for another moment.

Exhaling softly, he closed the bedroom door and headed back downstairs. If he was going to make breakfast he had to work quickly. Wade wouldn't allow Kristen to sleep much longer. He decided to make biscuits and sausage gravy for breakfast. He was taking the sausage out of the skillet when Kristen walked into the room holding Wade. His heart gave an extra thump at the sight they made together. She whispered something to Wade, which caused him to lift his head off her shoulder.

"Good morning, Daddy."

Randy smiled. "Good morning."

Kristen sat Wade down. "Breakfast smells good." She walked over to the stove and inhaled. "What's cooking?"

"Nothing now. I just finished and was getting ready to head upstairs to get you guys."

"Need any help?"

"Not with this, but you can help Wade into his booster seat."

Kristen sat Wade in his seat, and soon they were sitting around the table eating breakfast. Wade finished eating first, and Randy excused him from the table. Once he left the kitchen, Randy looked over at Kristen. "Did he surprise you this morning?"

Kristen took a sip of her milk. She swallowed before shaking her head. "Yes and no. He knocked so I had enough time to get my nightgown on."

Randy nodded, and Kristen sighed. "Do you think he is confused about us?"

Randy wasn't sure so he couldn't answer the question. "I don't know, but I would like to sit down and talk to him with you if you don't mind just to see what he thinks."

"Good idea."

He watched her take a sip of her milk. "When Wade knocked on the door this morning and announced himself, I looked for you. When I didn't see you, I reached for my nightgown and slipped it on then answered the door." She grinned. "Wade was standing there waiting. He didn't ask any questions. He just walked into the room and crawled into bed."

Kristen shrugged. "I figured it was something that he normally does with you so I crawled back in bed. Wade snuggled up to me, and we both fell asleep again."

She became quiet, and he gave her a concerned look. "What's wrong?"

She fidgeted, and he became nervous. Something was wrong. "What is it, Kristen?"

She sighed. "Yesterday he asked me if I was going to be his mother."

Randy choked on the coffee he just took a drink of. He wiped his mouth and had to clear his throat a few times before he could speak.

"What did you say?"

"You heard me right."

It was the last thing he expected to hear her say. He knew it was bound to come up at some point but not yet.

"What did you tell him?"

Kristen gave him a small smile. "I told him I would love to have him for a son, but there was no correct answer to that right now."

Randy nodded, satisfied with the answer, and he knew it had been an honest answer. He would like for Kristen to become his wife and the mother of his children. The fact that she seemed to be open to both options gave him hope. He could remember the distance and anger between them when she had come back to town for each of her grandfather's and grandmother's funerals. She had gone out of her way to ignore or avoid him. It had bothered him a lot, but he had never confided in anyone even though it seemed like everyone else had known anyway. His family members had been the main ones. His mother even made shameless attempts to reunite them, but it failed. It was his fault he been sucked in by Lila. Then again he wouldn't have Wade.

When he thought about his son, he hated her for what she put Wade through. In the beginning, he was upset about how she left him, but he knew that he had been unfair to Lila. She could never be a replacement for Kristen. He made demands of Lila that he knew she couldn't fulfill. Lila never had the desire to be a mother, but he chose to ignore it. In a way it was his fault, but Lila could have stayed for Wade's sake, even if she didn't want to be with him. Instead she left him to care for an infant son who still hadn't recovered from the loss. He hadn't heard from Lila since she left, and at this point, he didn't care to. Out of kindness, he took Wade to see Lila's aunt and uncle. They had also suffered because Lila had used them as well. She hadn't bothered to contact them since she left town.

He wondered if she ever thought about Wade. There was no way he could leave Wade behind and not think about him once. Closing his eyes, he rubbed his temples in an attempt to avoid the tension headache he could feel coming on. He looked up when Kristen cleared her throat.

"So when do you want to sit down and talk to Wade?"

"We can talk to him after we finish breakfast."

Kristen nodded, but he could see she was nervous. So was he because he had no idea what the outcome of the conversation was going to be, and he had good reason to be. He and Kristen had enough between them to work around. Closing his eyes he wondered when relationships had become so hard.

****

"I vote we go to Mandi's and do some shopping."

"My vote is we eat first and then we shop."

Kayla and Keirra turned to look at Kristen, and she rolled her eyes. They seemed to have this same argument every time, and she always had to be the tiebreaker.

"Normally, I wouldn't care, but I am hungry so I say we eat first and shop later."

To her surprise, no one grumbled, and they headed for the door. She had left Randy's after they had their talk with Wade. The talk had gone very well, and she would have stayed longer, but she and her sisters had already made plans. She locked the door and walked toward Keirra's car. They drove into town for Sam's Café. Keirra found them a good parking spot, and when they walked in. They waved at a few familiar people.

Kristen looked at her sisters. "Have you noticed a lot of the people we grew up with have left town?"

Keirra laughed. "None of the ones that needed to, but you must remember we left town."

Kristen grinned. "Yes, but now we are back."

Keirra gave her sisters a thoughtful look. "I wonder what it would take to get some of the others to come back."

Kayla's eyebrows rose. "Are you sure you want them to?"

After a quick contemplation, Keirra and Kristen shook their heads. The hostess came up to greet them before leading them to their table. Kristen picked up her menu and opened it.

"What are you going to have today, Kristen?"

She shrugged at Kayla not sure what she was going to have.

Keirra rolled her eyes. "You know you have tried just about everything on the menu."

Kristen smiled. "Well, variety is the spice of life."

She decided on the chicken and vegetable stir-fry. They smiled when Nadia came up to the table. They all placed their orders. She took their order, then moved on to the next table. Kristen turned to her sisters and began to fill them in on her interesting weekend. By the time Kristen was finished with her story, Kayla was laughing and Keirra was shaking her head in disbelief. Their food arrived so the conversation stalled while they ate a few bites of food.

"So I take this to mean you are back with Randy?"

Pausing in the middle of her bite, Kristen tried not to laugh at Keirra's surly expression. "I don't know."

Kayla gave her a surprised look. "What do you mean you don't know?"

Kristen shrugged. "We are seeing each other, but I wouldn't call it a relationship. We are just dating."

Sure she would like to be back with Randy, but she had to be realistic and not rush anything. She had enough experience in life to know that one's perception and the reality of things could differ.

She looked up at both of her sisters when she responded. "I am just taking my time. Randy and I still have a lot of things to work out." Kristen picked up her fork again. "Now let me try some of your manicotti."

Kayla gave her a warning look. "Don't think we didn't notice the way you changed the subject. The only thing I can say is do what it best for you. Take the time you need. There isn't any rush."

Kristen grinned. "Thank you, Kayla."

She stuck her fork into Kayla's plate and brought the fork back to her mouth. She moaned in pleasure when the pasta melted into her mouth. Kayla reached over and grabbed a bite of pepper steak from Keirra's plate. It was a ritual they had. All three of them had different tastes in food, but they still had to sample what the other had. An hour later, they paid their food bill and stood up.

Kristen grinned. "Now it is time to walk to Mandi's."

Keirra rubbed her stomach. "Sounds good to me. We can walk off some of this food we just ate."

Kayla nodded. "I am also thinking we should have gone shopping before we ate. I am positive I won't fit into anything I try on."

Keirra smiled. "Good. It means you will buy less, and we can go home sooner."

Kristen laughed as they walked out of the café and down the walkway. "Have you ever wondered why Sam calls Sam's Café a café when it is a restaurant?"

Kayla shrugged. "No, but I am sure he had his reasons."

All conversation ceased when Eric stepped out of the bakery and into their path. Kristen watched Keirra tense and sensed her sister had met her match. Greeting them, he gave them his heart-stopping grin. Kristen sighed when Keirra rolled her eyes and folded her arms across her chest. It was a sign that her sister intended to ignore him. Keirra had given her the same treatment several times over the years.

Kristen gave Eric an apologetic look. "How are you enjoying Baxley so far?"

He nodded. "I like it. It is a lot quieter than Atlanta."

Kristen smiled. "Have you settled in okay?"

Keirra cleared her throat "Can we be on our way?"

Kristen looked at Keirra in shock. Her sister had never been so rude. She gave Keirra an elbow.

Kristen gave Eric a polite smile. "It was nice to see you again. I'm sure we will see you around."

She shook her head when she heard Keirra mutter under her breath the feeling wasn't mutual.

"What was that about?" Kristen questioned as soon as they were out of earshot of Eric.

"Don't ask," Keirra grumbled. Kristen laughed, and they made their way into Mandi's clothing store.

* * * *

The trip back to the house was a short one, and Kristen collapsed into the recliner, and Kayla and Keirra fell onto the sofa.

Kristen groaned. "I am exhausted."

"So am I," Kayla replied with a heavy sigh.

Keirra grumbled. "Well I'm not. I have plenty of energy to burn."

Kayla snickered. "Give Eric a call. I am sure he can help you."

She barely managed to dodge the pillow Keirra threw at her.

Keirra stood with a frown on her face. "You aren't funny, Kayla."

She walked up the stairs, and Kristen began to laugh. "I think our sister has met her match."

Kayla chortled. "I know she has."

Kayla stood up and picked up her bag. "What I wonder is if I will meet my match anytime soon."

Kristen pulled herself into a standing position. "I am sure you will find someone who will challenge you."

Kayla headed for the stairs. "Well I am going to put my clothes away and clean up a little."

Kristen nodded and followed her sister up the stairs and detoured to her own room. She put up the two new skirts and shirts she bought before pulling out her outfit for work. It was a ritual she completed every night. She ironed the clothes because it would take five minutes off of the time it took for her to get ready. Taking her shower at night took another ten minutes, which she used to either sleep in or enjoy her breakfast a little longer. Once she had her outfit together, she hung it up and made her way to the shower. She put her hair up and then turned on the water and stepped into the shower.

She took a luxurious shower, not getting out until her skin threatened to wrinkle and become prune like. She turned off the water, stepped out of the shower then walked back into her bedroom and changed into her pajamas. She jumped when her cell phone rang. Looking at the caller ID, she smiled when Randy's name flashed on the screen.

"Hello."

"Hey, beautiful."

She sat down on the bed and tucked her feet up under her. "I wasn't expecting a call from you, but I always like to hear your voice."

"I know, but someone wanted to say something to you."

She heard the phone changing hands before Wade came on the line.

"Hi, Kristen. I had a good time this weekend. Good night, see you tomorrow."

She smiled when he rushed through the words. It was hard for her to reply because her throat had closed up with emotion. But she managed to reciprocate the feeling and waited for the phone to be handed back to Randy.

He came on the line a second later. "He wouldn't go to bed until I called you."

"Well he just made my night."

"I am glad. He likes you."

"I like him too."

"Well, I hate to rush, but I don't want to keep you long because I am sure you are getting ready for tomorrow and I need to get Wade into bed."

Kristen understood and said a quick good night. She hung up the phone and put it on the charger. Pulling back the covers, she crawled into bed and lay down. It was early, but she was tired and didn't have anything else to do.

Picking up the remote, she turned on the television. When she couldn't find anything good to watch, she turned to the reliable cartoon channel. It held her attention for the next hour and a half until she started to become sleepy. She set the timer on the television and reached for her teddy bear. Rolling onto her side, she closed her eyes and began to dream of Randy and Wade.

Chapter Ten

"Hey, Kristen, thanks for bringing me lunch."

Randy took the bag with Sam's Café logo on it out of her hands. Sometimes he hated working on Saturdays. He called her and told her he overslept this morning and had been in a rush to get Wade off to his mother's and in the process hadn't had time to make or pick up lunch. When he called, she had been in town taking care of errands and had been more than happy to pick up his lunch and drop it off. He requested a turkey sandwich with dill pickle slices, potato chips, and lemonade. She smiled when he opened the bag and pulled out the contents before he had the bag on the desk. He gave her a quick kiss then bit into a pickle.

"What time do you want me to come by your place for dinner tonight?"

He looked at the stack of paperwork on his desk before looking back at her. "Seven should be okay."

She nodded and turned to leave his office. "I will be there."

He sat down behind his desk. "Thanks again for lunch."

"You're welcome."

Kristen exited his office and ran right into Eric, who was leaning against the wall. She grinned knowing he had been waiting on her judging by his stance. Her smile widened when he tipped his hat to her. He hadn't been in Baxley long, but a few things had already rubbed off on him.

"How are you today, Kristen?"

"I'm fine and yourself?"

He chuckled. "Great thank you for asking."

They both stood there in silence until Eric cleared his throat. "Can you tell me something?"

She shrugged. "If I can tell you, I will."

"What does Keirra have against me?"

Kristen laughed and held up her hands. "I will answer your question to the best of my capability without having Keirra looking for me later. It isn't you. She doesn't like cops in general. If you want details you have to ask her."

Kristen readjusted the purse strap on her shoulder. "Keirra is going to be looking for blood just from me revealing that much."

She patted him on the shoulder. "You, my friend, are just going to have to be brave enough to ask her yourself."

Eric sighed. "I did ask her when I ran into her in town one day. She wouldn't say a word."

She knew the statement was literal. Keirra had a way of shutting down that was hard to describe, but if she didn't want to talk, she wouldn't say another word.

Kristen gave him a sympathetic look. "I will give you another hint to deal with my sister. It is always better to challenge her. Keirra loves competition and can't stand to lose."

Knowing she had given Eric enough to think about, she turned and left the building. She got into her car and drove off to her hair appointment. Hopefully Eric would contemplate what she told him for a little while before confronting Keirra because then she would have a confrontation of her own.

* * * *

Randy looked up when Eric knocked on his door, and he waved him in. He was in the middle of a bite of sandwich, but he motioned for Eric to sit while he chewed.

"How is it going?"

Eric took a seat and nodded. "All is well in love and war."

Randy looked at him with raised eyebrows. "What do you mean?"

Eric just smiled. "What can you tell me about Keirra and how to challenge her?"

Randy leaned back in his chair and interlaced his fingers. "So you like Keirra?"

Eric grinned. "I do."

Randy leaned forward. "First, you have to understand her, and I have to tell you that as long as I have known Keirra, I still don't understand her one hundred percent."

Eric chuckled. "You're right. How would you describe Keirra?"

Randy laughed. "I have one word for you, complex."

Eric frowned. "Why doesn't she like cops?"

Randy held his hands up. "It isn't my place to tell you."

Eric laughed. "You know, I find it very strange that every time I ask that question, I get same response."

Randy smiled. "I'm not surprised. Now, I won't lie, I'm not afraid of most women, but Keirra is one of the few I am afraid of. She can tear a person to pieces with her tongue-lashing. I also don't spread people's business."

Eric nodded. There was a confused expression on his face. Randy took the last bite of his sandwich then looked in his drawer for a peppermint. He popped one in his mouth and leaned back in his chair.

"Besides, I have my own issues to figure out between me and Kristen."

Eric gave him an inquisitive look. "What is up between you and Kristen? The two of you seem to have a lot of chemistry."

Randy sighed. "Twelve years of chemistry, but I messed it up six years ago. I made the mistake of doubting our relationship, and now I am struggling to get it back."

Eric looked at him in surprise. "I had no idea you and Kristen had been an item so long."

Randy rubbed the back of his neck. "We would still be an item if I hadn't screwed up. I broke up with Kristen for what I thought was a logical reason at the time. But I can tell you in hindsight I was just being stupid and immature."

Eric gave him a curious look. "Why did you break up?"

"Because I thought she was kissing another guy."

Eric gave him a confused look. "You thought she was kissing another guy?"

Randy sat up straight. "To make a long story short I saw her kissing another guy and jumped to the conclusion that she was cheating on me. So I broke up with her. Turns out the guy was forcing himself on her, and I walked in at the wrong time and walked out at the wrong time."

Eric frowned. "What do you mean?"

"I missed her slapping the guy for pushing himself on her. He was some guy who liked her, but she didn't like him. He found out the hard way, and so did I."

Eric shook his head. "Man, that is tough."

Randy sighed in frustration. "More than you know. You have no idea what it is like to sit back and watch the woman that you have cared so much about doubt the entire time you were together. It kills me. I made the biggest mistake in my life, and I'm not sure that I will ever be able to make it right."

"You are Kristen are together, right?"

Randy shook his head. "I don't know how to explain it, man. We are together, yet we're not. I guess you could call it dating, but I want more than that. I want it to go back to the way things were, but I'm not sure that it can."

Eric gave him a grim look. "It sounds like you have your work cut out for you."

Randy sighed. "You're right, but she is worth it. Kristen is a good person. She is a good woman. Kristen has always brought out the good in me. I didn't realize how happy I was with her until we weren't together anymore."

Eric gave him a sympathetic smile. "Don't sell yourself short. I haven't known you long, but you seem like a good guy. Kristen must think so as well, or she wouldn't be giving you another chance."

Randy nodded realizing that Eric had a point. "I hadn't thought about it like that before now, but you are right."

Eric stood up. "The only question I have for you, is are you asking for the impossible?"

Randy looked up at Eric with puzzlement. "What do you mean?"

"It seems that you are concerned with things being the way they were in the past between you and Kristen, but it may not be possible. I'm sure that you and Kristen are different people now than you were back then. The relationship may never go back to being the same because neither of you are."

Staring at Eric, he digested the words. Eric had a good point. He and Kristen were different people. Maybe he was focused on the wrong thing. He was so busy trying to rekindle their old relationship he hadn't given any thought to building a new relationship. A different relationship based upon the people they had become.

* * * *

"Can I take the blindfold off now?"

"No."

Impatient, Kristen huffed, which was abnormal for her, but she had been blindfolded since they had left the restaurant. It seemed like an hour ago, but she wasn't sure how long it had been. She had been led to his truck, and he had driven somewhere. She was all for surprises, but this was pushing it. Once they stopped, he picked her up and carried her into his house, although she was guessing because she was sitting on what seemed to be a bed.

"How about now?"

Randy chuckled. "Ask one more time, and you will have the blindfold on all night." He paused for a second. "Although, it might not be a bad idea."

Kristen grumbled, and he gave her a brief kiss on the lips before leaving the room again. She heard a door close, and muffled sound followed. Seconds later, she felt his presence, and he reached behind her and untied the blindfold. The sight in front her was breathtaking. She had guessed right. She was in his bedroom, but it had been transformed into a bedroom for seduction. Candles were lit and placed in the right areas to give off enough light for her to see. Rose petals trailed from where she sat on the bed and led to the bathroom. He held out his hand to her, and she took it. He led her to the bathroom, and she gasped.

The bathroom was lit with candles, and a trail of rose petals led across the floor and up the steps to his sauna tub. Rose petals floated on top of the water, and Kristen turned to face him. Stretching upward, she placed a kiss on his lips. When he pulled back, she smiled.

"Was it worth the wait?"

She tilted her head to side in a playful fashion. "That remains to be seen."

His hands came up and grabbed the hem of her shirt, and he pulled it over her head. She brought her hands up to lift her hair while he slid her skirt down over her hips. Once it pooled on the floor, she stepped out of it, and he knelt before her. He slipped her shoes off of her feet. His underwear followed, and when she was nude, he stood and her hands went to his shirt. Once she had the buttons undone, she slid the shirt off his shoulders. She knelt in front of him and his boots came off, followed by his pants.

He stood clad in his boxer briefs, yet his erection was already fighting to get free. She stripped him of the briefs, and he picked her up. She wrapped her legs around his waist. He stepped into the tub with her and sat down. She moaned when the warm water surrounded them.

"What made you think of something like this?"

Randy smiled. "A little conversation with Kayla."

Kristen placed her head on his shoulder and exhaled softly. "Remind me to thank Kayla later."

He chuckled. "Sure."

Leaning back, he ran his hand up and down her back. "Are you comfortable?"

She unwrapped herself from around him and turned around. He opened his legs, and she settled between them. His hands came up to her shoulders and began to massage her tense muscles. She moaned, letting her head drop forward.

"That feels good."

He didn't respond. Instead, he kept massaging her shoulders. Following the curve of her spine, he slid his hands lower. He placed a kiss on the back of her neck, and she moaned again. His hands came up in front of her, and his fingertips brushed her breasts, before cupping them in his palms. He paid special attention to her nipples, and she gasped as heat pooling between her thighs. His hand trailed lower, brushing her stomach and then her thighs. A cry of pleasure escaped her when his hands found the heat between her thighs. He began to stroke her in a slow but steady pace, a few heartbeats later she gripped his thighs and cried out her release.

"No fair," she gasped.

She felt his smile against her neck in response. "Yes, it is. This night is for you."

She turned to face him, and his mouth came down on hers. His kiss was light and teasing.

He deepened the kiss, and she opened her mouth and felt his tongue slip inside. She applied a little suction, and he pulled away with a moan of pleasure.

"You are going to make this hard for me, aren't you?"

She wiggled against him a little and gave him a wicked look. "I think it already is."

He reached behind her and pulled the stopper out of the drain. It was a good thing he put the extra drainer in there. He stood up pulling her with him. He reached for a towel and wrapped her in it, then reached for another and wrapping it around his waist. He stepped out of the tub and onto the rug. Bending his knees, he lifted her up into his arms. She enjoyed the sight because she could see his muscles ripple. He carried her from the bathroom and into the bedroom and sat her on the bed.

"Don't move."

She watched as he went into the bathroom and figured he was blowing out the candles since the light was starting to fade. He emerged a few minutes later, and she smiled, flattered that he was willing to put together something so romantic for her. She watched him come toward her. The man was sexy, too sexy. He surprised her when he continued by her instead of stopping in front of her.

The lamp came on, and she blinked at the obtrusive glare. "This is the only time the lamp will come on tonight."

He held a box in his hand. It was a jewelry box, and she became nervous until she realized it was too big to be a ring box. He placed it in her hands.

"Open it."

She took the box with hands sturdier than they should be and gasped after she opened it. A gold locket lay inside the jewelry box. She took it out of the box, and when she realized it opened, she flipped the locket open. Tears came to her eyes, and she placed her hand over her mouth. The locket contained a picture of her and Randy on their third date. They had been at a carnival, and it had been one of her favorite dates. He took the necklace out of her hand and opened the clasp.

She was still while he slipped the locket around her neck. She brought her hand up to hold it. "When did you get this?"

"About a month before you were scheduled to graduate from college."

She looked at him in surprise. "It was your graduation present."

He gave a brief nod, and she gave him a gentle smile. "You are wonderful. Thank you for the locket. I like it."

"I am glad."

He scooped her up and laid her back on the bed. Lying down beside her, he turned off the lamp and then pulled her into his arms. His lips came down on hers. He pulled back and looked deep into her eyes. "I hate that I didn't give it to you on your graduation night."

She placed a finger to his lips. "Better late than never. Now kiss me."

Chapter Eleven

Kristen moaned in pleasure when Randy's lips met hers. She had only expected dinner with Randy and Wade tonight. It had been a good dinner. She was able to keep her promise to Wade, and they cooked together. Randy had surprised her when he allowed her to participate in Wade's bedtime routine. After Randy gave a Wade a bath he carried him to his bedroom where she was waiting. She tucked Wade in and read him a story before kissing him good night.

The simple gesture meant a lot to her, but she didn't have time to ponder her emotions because as soon as Randy closed the door to Wade's room, he tugged her into his embrace. He led her to his bedroom and undressed both of them. Now there wasn't an inch of her body he didn't touch or taste. From the tender spot on her neck to the sensitive spot on the curve where her back and bottom met were lavished with attention. She was putty in his hands by the time he turned her over. Yet, when his mouth found her sensitive entrance, she bit her lips to mute her cry of pleasure and arched into him.

It didn't take long for her to go over the edge. Randy was so talented with his mouth and knew which spot to hit to drive her insane with pleasure. He held her close while the tremors raced through her and then reached protection. When she was able to catch her breath, he entered her, and they both moaned at the intense feeling. They clung to each other, enjoying the feel of him inside of her.

They last contractions of her pleasure caused him to move. That was all it took to shatter his control and for his body to take over. He began to move, each thrust deeper and more pleasurable than the last until she was clinging to him overrun with desire. He groaned into the pillow when he felt her begin to contract around his. Her pleasure took him over the brink, and his sound of pleasure vibrated in her ear muffled by the pillow. When they were both able to breathe without gasping, Kristen began to laugh.

"We should have taken Wade to your mom's."

Randy lifted his head and looked her at her. There was a sated smile on his face. "He's okay. We were quiet. Besides, if you and I are together, we can't take him over to my mom's house every time we want to make love."

She studied him carefully. He was right, and she nodded. "You are right. We just have to be careful."

He rolled away from her, and she instantly missed his warmth. "I will be right back."

She reached for the blanket while she watched him walk away from the bed. The man was so sexy it was unreal. *How she had gotten so lucky?*

Randy returned quickly and she saw the front side looked as good as his backside. He rejoined her in bed and pulled her into his arms. She rested her head against his chest thinking about the upcoming weekend.

"Do you think your mom and dad will like their anniversary gift?"

Randy nodded. "They're going to love it."

Kristen smiled. It was easy to shop for his parents because she knew them so well. Tomorrow was their anniversary, and everyone was getting together to celebrate it. It was a surprise party, but for some reason, she didn't think the Strouds were going to be too surprised. From what she could remember, Mr. and Mrs. Stroud always expected a party, but she was spending the night with Randy so she could help him prepare a few last-minute things needed for the party.

She was so excited about the anniversary party that when Randy woke her up the next morning, she rolled out of bed. She helped Randy set up for the party before rushing to get dressed. It had been a long time since she had been in the presence of all of the Strouds. She slipped into a rose-colored, spaghetti-strapped sundress and the flat sandals that matched. Walking into the bathroom, she began fixing her hair, deciding she was going to wear it up. She began to twist it up and pin it until she had it tamed and designed.

Randy came into the room just as she finished. The look in his eyes spoke of trouble, and she backed up from him. "Don't even think about it."

He stepped closer anyway. "But you look so good."

She laughed. "According to you, I always look good, but I don't have time to get wrinkled."

His expression became devilish. "Who says you are going to get wrinkled?"

His arms encircled her, but the doorbell rang, and she sighed with relief "I guess this just wasn't meant to be," she teased.

She sneaked around him, avoiding his hands before heading down the stairs and to the front door. When she opened it, Cody and his family stood on the other side of the door. She embraced them.

"You still look as beautiful as ever, Kristen. I used to be jealous of my brother when I saw you two together, but you two belong together," Cody whispered to her.

She smiled when he pulled back and did not bother to correct Cody. The last thing she wanted to do was get into a long, drawn-out conversation trying to clarify what she and Randy were. "Thank you, and I have missed you too. You have a beautiful family."

Cody Jr. reached for her when they were introduced. When she went to hand him back to his mother and was surprised when he clung to her. She looked at Randy with surprise, and he just shrugged. She resettled Cody Jr. on her hip. She didn't mind holding him as long as he wanted. Her gaze went to Randy, and she wondered if he would be the one she would have children with.

Randy smiled before he embraced his brother.

"It seems I may have to battle my nephew for my woman."

Cody laughed. "Well, if you do, you will have fight on your hands."

Kristen struggled to keep her expression clear. Did Randy consider her to be his woman? She sighed when she realized it was just one more thing they needed to discuss. Right now, she liked the arrangement they had. They were getting to know each other again, and she was trying to see Randy for the man that he was and not the man he used to be. Gone was the predictable boy she knew. In his place stood a complex man she had to get to know all over again. The same could be said for her. She was no longer naïve and idealistic. She focused on the reality of the situation at hand. The problem was she was still trying to figure out what was in front of her. However, today wasn't the day to do it. It was Ophelia and Spencer's anniversary party. She and Randy could wait until later. If she had been able to wait six years, she could wait a few more hours.

She closed the door and asked everyone if they wanted anything to drink. She left for the kitchen to fill the drink orders, and when she returned with the drinks, the doorbell was ringing again. Randy stood to answer it, and Blair and Drake were standing there. There was more embracing and greeting from everyone because Blair did live off by herself.

After spending some time with Drake, she knew Blair was more than okay with him. The fact he was an attractive man didn't hurt either. Randy went and got the drinks for his sister and Drake while she handed out the ones she had to Cody and Alexandra. Once Randy returned with the drinks, everyone settled in. His sister Emily and her family arrived prior to Randy's parents did. She realized a lot had changed. For some reason, she never imagined Cody and Emily so grown up. Cody was three years younger than her, and Emily was the same age as her and her sisters, but she still couldn't imagine them at the point where they were in their lives. Yet, here they were sitting in front of her. Kristen looked down at Cody Jr. and Tracey since both had been fighting for her affection since they arrived. She favored Emily. Kristen looked over at Randy who was smiling at her.

"I think you have two fans."

She smiled and shrugged. "I guess I do."

The only time the two children had been off of her lap was to eat. Emily and Cody's children were adorable. Another thing she noticed was Wade loved his Aunt Blair. He hadn't left her side since she and her fiancé, Drake, had arrived. She was almost starting to feel neglected.

"Okay, Mom and Dad, it's time for you two to open your gifts."

Randy stood, and Emily grabbed Tracey while Cody grabbed Cody Jr. Kristen watched the Strouds receive present after present. Their grandchildren were more than happy to help them with the presents. Kristen watched them enjoying the interaction. It was occasions like this she missed. Occasions like this she longed for.

"I am so glad you and Randy are back together."

Uncertain of how to respond, she looked at Blair. Kristen smiled. "We're not together."

Blair gave her a stunned look. "But I thought . . ."

She reached for Blair's hand. "Randy and I are trying to work through things."

Blair sighed. "Well, I hope you and Randy can work it out. The two of you are good together, and it is good to have you with us again."

"I have missed you guys a lot, and I know we have a lot to catch up on."

Blair smiled. "We do."

Blair shifted Wade in her lap. "How are your sisters doing?"

Kristen grinned. "They are doing very well. Both of them were supposed to be here today, but Kayla had already made plans, and Keirra wasn't feeling well this morning. Kayla might be able to come by a little later."

"Well we won't be leaving until tomorrow afternoon. Maybe we can meet up sometime before then."

Kristen nodded because she knew her sisters were looking forward to seeing all of the Strouds again. They had grown up with them, and there had been nothing but good times.

"Thank you for the gift, Kristen."

She looked up when Ophelia leaned down to hug her. "You're welcome."

"Be sure to thank Kayla and Keirra for me."

"I will."

The rest of the party was fun. When it was time for everyone to leave, she felt a sense of sadness fall over her. She hated for the fun to end, but she knew it wouldn't be the last time she and all of the Strouds would get together.

Randy's brother and sisters all embraced her repeating they were glad to see her and they were looking forward to seeing her again. She returned the sentiment before everyone leave. They were all going to spend the night at their parents' house then leave out tomorrow. She and Randy had insisted a few of them stay at the house, but they claimed they didn't want to impose. They were allowed to leave with the promise someone would come back if everyone didn't fit comfortably in the house. Kristen knew even while Randy spoke the words that no one would take them up on the offer. The Strouds had a lot of room at their house. They were supposed to meet up at the house in the morning to have breakfast. Randy closed the door when his last sibling pulled out of the driveway.

He turned to look at her and Wade. "Well that went very well."

Wade nodded. "Yes, Kristen did good."

Kristen laughed at Wade. Randy narrowed his eyes, but she saw him fighting a laugh himself. He took his son out of her arms and tossed him up in the air.

"Just for that comment someone will be washing the dishes all by himself."

Wade groaned. "I can't reach the sink."

Randy carried him into the kitchen. "Well, you had better grow a couple of inches and quick."

Kristen followed them into the kitchen, and a short time, they had the dishwasher loaded and the kitchen cleaned. By the time she made it upstairs, Randy had Wade in the bathtub. She went into his bathroom and took a quick shower and changed into her nightgown. Knowing Wade was going to be joining them for a little while, she put her robe on. By the time she entered the bedroom Wade was already in the middle of the bed.

He scooted over to make room for her. She slid in beside him and Randy. He had removed his shirt and shoes. She followed him with her eyes all the way to the bed. Wade handed her the remote control to the television. She took it and turned the television on and switched it to the Disney Channel. Wade made it through one kid show and then fell asleep, like she knew he would. Randy lifted him up and went to place him in his own bed. Randy returned to the room closing and locking the door before rejoining her in bed and pulling her underneath him.

She laughed, and he smiled. "What are you doing?"

The look in his eyes became heated. "I am going to finish what I had planned for us this morning."

The heat in her own gaze increased while her smile faded. "Go ahead and do your worst."

When Randy's lips touched hers all thoughts left her mind, and the only thing that mattered was Randy making love to her.

* * * *

"I am so excited about seeing all of your family again."

Keirra mumbled something around a sip of coffee that sounded like an agreement with Kayla's statement. All of them had their own fond memories. Kristen had been able to talk her sisters into coming over to the Strouds for breakfast.

Randy had convinced everyone to ride together. Being his idea, he was the one who had to pick up everyone. She and her sisters had all brought something to go with breakfast. When the front door to the Strouds' residence swung open, an excited Emily stood there. She and Keirra embraced for what felt like a year before Randy broke up the reunion and ushered everyone inside.

With the arrival of Kristen and her sisters everyone soon became excited. Soon breakfast was ready, and everyone was sitting around the table catching up. Wendy, Cody. Jr., and Tracey were introduced, and the confusion on their face of seeing three women who looked alike was amusing. Kristen liked that

Wade was able to tell her apart from her sisters even though there hadn't been too many times when all three of them had been present when he was around. Even with all of the excitement, Kristen felt an overwhelming sense of sadness. It was gatherings like this that made her feel sorrow. She missed the good times with her family.

Feeling the onslaught of tears coming, she excused herself from the table. She stepped out onto the front porch and wiped the tears from her face. The front door opened a second later, but she kept her back to the person who had joined her. Randy's arms encircled her, and she leaned back into him.

"What's wrong?"

Unable to speak, Kristen shook her head. Tears began to flow faster, and when she could no longer disguise her crying, she turned and pressed her face into Randy's chest. He comforted her until she was able to compose herself. She smiled when he produced a napkin.

"Thank you," she mumbled when he led her to the porch swing.

He brushed away a tear. "Do you want to talk about it?"

Kristen looked up at Randy and gave him a sad look. "Every once in a while something happens to remind me of the times we spent with Mom, Dad, Nana, and Grandpa, and I get a little upset."

Randy grinned. "Is there anything I can do?"

Kristen shook her head. "Being here for me right now is enough. It might sound strange, but I enjoy the memories even when they are sad."

Randy placed a kiss on her forehead and pulled her closer. He held her until she was ready to go back inside. When they went back in, they retook their seats. A quick glance at her sisters told Kristen they knew what was on her mind, and Kayla, who was sitting on the other side of her, squeezed her hand.

"Just think about the good times."

Kristen nodded and took a deep breath. When she looked up she almost gasped out loud. The Strouds were no longer in front of her. Instead, it was her mother, father, and maternal grandparents surrounding her. She almost felt like she was in a dream state. Her mother smiled at her, and she returned one of her own. When her mother spoke, she couldn't hear her but she read her mother's lips. A strong sense of calmness came over her, and when she blinked, the room came back into focus, and the Strouds and her sisters were before her. Kayla squeezed her hand again, and a genuine smile came to Kristen's face. She was going to be okay. The family she needed right now was around her.

Chapter Eleven

Kristen let out a loud whoop of joy, and her sisters looked at her like she had lost her mind when she walked into the living room.

Keirra's expression was full of annoyance. "What is all the noise about?"

"Grandma and Grandpa are coming into town tomorrow."

Keirra beamed. "That is great."

Kayla frowned. "When will they arrive? I need to clean the house up before they arrive. Do you know how long are they going to stay?"

Kristen laughed, and then she shrugged. "The house is clean enough, Kayla. We aren't slobs, and you know you can never put a time limit on Grandma and Grandpa. They are free spirits coming and going as they please."

Her sisters nodded. They were used to their grandparents' extensive traveling, which made them enjoy their infrequent visits even more. Kristen grinned at the thought of her father's parents coming into town. She loved to see them, especially her grandfather because it was like seeing her dad all over again. She looked down at her cell phone when it rang and smiled at Randy's number.

"Hello."

"Hey, sweetheart, I'm calling to let you know I'm turning onto your street."

She grabbed her pursed. "Okay. I am ready and walking out the door now."

"You can wait for me inside so I can say hi to your sisters. Besides, a gentleman doesn't sit in the car and blow his horn at a lady."

She laughed. "Okay, Randy. See you soon."

She disconnected the call and looked at her sisters. "I will help you clean and fix up the guest room when I get in tonight."

Keirra chortled. "You might want to make sure they are going to sleep in the house first. They could just park the RV on the front lawn and stay in it."

Kayla shook her head, and then frowned at Keirra. "I will be sure to tell them you said that." She stood and looked at Kristen. "Don't worry about rushing back to help. I will take care of it. You just go out and enjoy yourself."

Kristen smiled at her sisters. "I always do."

The doorbell rang cutting off Kayla's reply. Kristen opened the door to find Randy standing on the other side looking handsome. He gave her a brief kiss then stepped inside to greet her sisters. After a brief conversation, she and Randy left.

He led her to his truck, and she was assailed by the smell of pizza after he opened the door. She looked over at Randy when he slid inside the truck.

"Is that Jimmy's Pizza?"

Randy nodded, and she moaned in anticipation. She loved Jimmy's pizza. Since she and her sisters had been back in Baxley, they had eaten Jimmy's Pizza a few times, but the pizza was so heavy, and so good, eating it too often was pure gluttony. Randy drove to his house. She smiled when he reached into the back seat and pulled the pizza out. He climbed out of the truck before going around to her side and opening her door. He led the way inside and straight toward the backyard. Citronella candles were lit, but her eyes were drawn to the blanket in the middle of the yard. A telescope was set up not too far from it.

She looked at him in surprise. "Are we stargazing?"

"And eating Jimmy's Pizza."

She laughed. "I remember the last time we did this."

"It was a long time ago."

She looked at him. "Yes, but a lot of times, it seems like it was just yesterday."

He led her to the blanket holding her hand with his free hand and carrying the pizza in the other. She sat down on the blanket first, and he handed her the pizza then reached into his back pockets. He placed packets of crushed pepper and Parmesan cheese on the blanket. Reaching into his other pocket he pulled out napkins. She watched him lower his frame onto the blanket beside her. He pulled off his shoes and socks before reaching for her feet. Since she had worn sandals he didn't have much work to do. Once they were comfortable, she opened the pizza box and dug in. The first delicious slice had a lot of cheese and grease, just the way she liked it. She took a bite and moaned. "This is great."

He took his first bite nodding in agreement. "Tell me about it."

She gave him a bright smile. "Grandma and Grandpa are going to be in town tomorrow."

His lips curved upward. "That's cool. It has been a while since I have seen them."

"It has been about six months since we have seen them."

"What's bringing them through town?"

Kristen shrugged. "Who knows? You know they come and go when they please. They have worked hard all of their lives and are retired now. They deserve to roam the country if it makes them happy."

There was one time of the year she knew she would always see her father's parents and that was the anniversary of their father's death. It was a time when they got together and shared the good times and stories about their father. The anniversary was a time for them to catch up with everything going on in each other's lives.

He picked up the last slice of pizza after making sure she didn't want it. "What do you guys have planned?"

She shrugged. "To be honest, I have no idea, but whatever it is, I would like for you and Wade to be involved."

Randy smiled. "I like that idea, and I am sure Wade will, too."

She grinned. "Good. I am sure my grandparents would like to see you again."

At least they should. There were a lot of activities going on in Baxley this week due the fact homecoming was this weekend. It was going to be a good game. Different dances and celebrations were going on around the town. It was a fun time in Baxley so her grandparents were coming through at a good time.

He reached out and gave her a hand a light squeeze. "Well, either way I'm sure it will be a good time."

Kristen nodded before looking up at the sky. It was so clear out she didn't need the telescope. Randy finished off the last slice of pizza and cleaned his hands, then took her into his arms.

He lay back, and they began to debate over which constellation they were staring at. Kristen was sure he made up a few along the way, but it was so much fun she didn't care.

She looked up at Randy loving the relaxed feel of being with him.

"Randy where are we going with this?"

He replied without hesitation. "I don't know, Kristen. I know where I would like for this to go, but it is up to you."

He studied her carefully while she thought about what he said. She sighed, and he tilted her head toward his. His lips found hers. The affection she felt behind his kiss made her heart swell with an emotion hard to describe. The one thing she knew was she cared about Randy more this time around than she did last time, but was it enough? She was taking it slow. She just hoped she wasn't setting herself up for another painful heartbreak.

Pulling back, she looked up at Randy. "I'm scared."

He gave her a gentle look. "Why?"

She sighed and looked away from him. "I'm afraid you will hurt me again. You have no idea what our breakup did to me."

He gave her a sad look. "You're right. I don't know, but I want you to tell me."

She was quiet for a long time, uncertain of where she should start. She exhaled the pent-up breath she was holding and closed her eyes. "I was devastated when you broke up with me, Randy. Besides my sisters, you were everything to me. Even when I was off in college we worked hard to keep our relationship the same. I thought everything was okay."

Kristen opened her eyes and looked at Randy. "When you broke up with me, I didn't know what to do. It felt like a part of me had been ripped away. I was confused, upset, depressed. I tried to figure out what I'd done wrong, but I couldn't."

She exhaled a shaky breath. "You wouldn't return my calls. You wouldn't give me an answer to why. I thought you found someone else and decided you no longer wanted to be with me."

She looked away from him. "Keirra talked to Emily, and when Emily told her that you weren't involved with anyone else, it hurt. I thought it was me, and it hurt to think that you just didn't want to be with me."

Tears came to her eyes as her words reopened the pain. She tried to blink them back. "It took me a long time to recover, Randy, and as we sit here, I'm not sure that I have. It took me a long time to get back the joy that I felt when I was with you. I don't want to lose that joy again. Even if it means that I can never be with you again."

The pain that she saw on Randy's face matched what she felt. The words she spoke were true. She couldn't allow Randy to hurt her the way he did when he broke up with her the first time. She had to protect herself this time. It would hurt not to be with Randy, but it would hurt a lot more if she allowed him back into her life and he decided to push her out of his life again. It was a risk she couldn't take.

* * * *

"Grandma, Grandpa!"

Kristen stepped forward to embrace her grandparents. She had been looking forward to their arrival all morning. Each of them hugged her before stepping inside the house and embracing Kayla and Keirra. A quick look outside showed her grandparents had parked their RV in the driveway and not on the lawn like Keirra had suggested they would. She gave Keirra a smug look, and Keirra smiled when she stepped forward to greet their grandparents.

"We are so glad you could make it."

Kristen went and stood by Randy and Wade. Wade held his arms up to her, and she picked him up and loved the feel of him in her arms. She waited until he grandparents had finished talking to Kayla and Keirra before introducing Randy and Wade to her grandparents. They were happy to see Randy as she predicted, and her grandparents found Wade adorable. He became the person of the hour, but a short while later, they headed out of the house and loaded into Randy's truck.

Miraculously they all were able to fit and had a little room to spare. They decided to eat at Sam's because it had a little bit of what everyone wanted. They were seated, orders were taken and the pictures came out. Her grandparents began sharing the photos of their recent travels and funny stories were spread around the table. Kristen sat back and watched her family. She loved times like these because she didn't feel so alone. There were times she was starved for family. Not that her sisters didn't count, but the pain of not having a mother and father made her cherish her surviving grandparents even more.

She planned on talking to her grandparents about visiting and calling more often. Family was important and having their surviving family near would help. It was another thing that hurt about her breakup with Randy. If they had stayed together she knew they would have the family that she always dreamed of.

"What are you thinking about?"

She looked over at Randy when he spoke to her. The fact he always seemed to know when something was on her mind was cute to her. He insisted her eyes always gave her away. She knew that was true. It was something she inherited from her father. When she was a little girl she could look into her father's eyes and know what he was thinking. Even the night he had been shot, he told them he was okay, but she had been able to read the fear and the pain in his eyes. At the time, she hadn't known what the expression in his eyes had meant, but in the end, she realized her father had known he wasn't going to be with them much longer. It had been something she had never forgotten. She looked up when Randy reached over and squeezed her hand.

"Whatever it is it is going to be okay."

She smiled at him and nodded. "You are right. It will be okay."

The last thing she wanted to do was ruin a happy occasion by thinking sad thoughts, so she turned her attention back to her grandparents and laughed at her grandmother's reenactment of her grandfather's run-in with a raccoon. It seemed her grandfather could move quicker than it looked.

Their food arrived, and they ate, and then it was their turn to share their stories of anything interesting that occurred lately. Of course, the highlight of the subject was Keirra fighting her attraction to Eric. Even Randy teased her until the point Keirra threatened to leave Baxley for good. Everyone let up, but the conversation became serious the next time their grandmother spoke.

"Keirra, you shouldn't let what happened to your father get in the way of having a good healthy relationship."

Her grandmother leaned back in her chair and stared at Keirra. "Personally, I think your father would have a fit if he knew you were acting like this."

Keirra went to deny the claim, but their grandmother interrupted. "Tell me this. Would you feel the way you do about police officers if your father had lived?"

The question made Keirra gasp with shock, but their grandmother continued on. "I hope your answer would still be the same because the danger would still be there."

Kristen looked over at Randy. She knew the risk she was taking by dating an officer of the law, but for some reason it didn't bother her. What scared her more was their relationship hadn't worked out before because Randy hadn't had faith in her feelings for him. She looked at him across the table and wondered if that had changed.

Chapter Twelve

Kristen leaned back and groaned in misery. She was miserable for two reasons. The first was she was sitting at Sam's Café, and the second she had gorged herself.

"This is the last time we eat at Sam's . . . at least this year."

Kayla laughed then groaned. "Don't fool yourself. We have three months to go. There is no way we will make it."

They both looked over at Keirra who was still eating. She was a slow eater. Sometimes it was a good thing, and other times it was a bad thing. Right now, it was a bad thing because they had to sit in Sam's for a longer time and stare at their food longer. Kristen took a last look at her herb stuffed grilled chicken and pushed it away. Kayla did the same with her lasagna. Sure enough, she wasn't able to help herself. She picked up her fork and took another bite of Keirra's Oriental Beef Stir Fry.

"Okay, now I'm really done."

Kayla rubbed her stomach. "I've gained ten pounds since I have been back."

Kristen shook her head. "Impossible. You look just fine. I doubt you have even gained two."

Kristen looked over at her sister. She had a healthy glow about her. They all did. Being back in Baxley was good for all of them. Everybody looked relaxed and happy.

Kayla yawned. "So what time does the bonfire start?"

Keirra sat up "Seven, and the dance will start when it's over."

Baxley High was playing Graham High, and it was an event that brought a large crowd. Everyone in Baxley participated. Baxley and Graham could be considered archrivals, but it wasn't a serious issue. It was just a reason for the city to get together and have a good time. It also gave Baxley a reason to brag if they won.

Kayla laughed. "We need to get a move on then. It is going to take Keirra an hour to get ready."

Keirra grumbled. "No longer than it will take you. I'm sure."

Kristen stood up and shook her head. "Come on, you two."

Kristen had to admit Kayla was right, which was why she had pushed the issue of Keirra getting her clothes ready before they ate. The ploy had worked so it should cut down on the time needed to get ready. They paid for their food and walked to her car.

"Does anyone need to stop anywhere?"

With two simultaneous no's, Kristen drove toward the house. She would take a quick nap and then get dressed. A short time later, she pulled up in the driveway, and they all piled out of the car and into the house.

"Have you heard from Grandma or Grandpa," Kayla asked when she sat down on the sofa.

"Not yet, but I will call them when I wake up from my nap and find out for certain."

Their grandparents had left earlier that morning on their way to their next destination. She smiled. They had a major traveling bug. Their excuse was they wanted to get all of their traveling out of the way before they had to settle down when their great-grandkids started to come along. Kristen turned, walked up the stairs, and went up to her bedroom. She set her alarm for thirty minutes and took off her shoes then lay down.

When her head touched the pillow she fell asleep, but the alarm still went off too soon. Groaning in exhaustion she sat up, swinging her legs over of the edge of the bed. Sticking her head out the door she called out to Keirra. Keirra opened her bedroom door and looked out.

"What time are you leaving?"

Keirra shrugged. "In the next two hours."

"Okay."

Kristen went back in her room and moved toward the closet. Flipping through her clothes, she chose a hot pink gypsy skirt that stopped just below her knees and black turtle neck sweater. She would finish the outfit with her pink ankle-high boots. She took out all the items and placed them on the bed. She headed for her bathroom. After turning on the water, she stepped into the shower. She soaked for a while then began to bathe. Not wanting to stay in too long, she turned off the water and dried off.

She walked back into her room and began to get ready. Once she was dressed, she pulled her hair up into a clip and let the ends fall around her face. Satisfied with the look she applied light makeup and then grabbed her bottle of pink nail polish to do a brush up on her hands, waving and blowing on them to speed up the drying process. She slid into her shoes before walking over to the full-length mirror. After a full turn before the mirror, she sprayed on perfume, grabbed her purse, and went downstairs.

Kayla was already downstairs, and Kristen let out a wolf-whistle of appreciation. Kayla looked good in the dress she picked out to wear. It had been a while since she had seen Kayla wear the dress. Keirra came downstairs a little while later, and Kristen and Kayla's mouths dropped. The off-the-shoulder dress she was wearing must have been bought in secret. Keirra didn't wear dresses. She said they were only made to torture women like pantyhose. A skirt on occasion, but never a dress—either way, Keirra looked hot.

She was going to compliment Keirra, but she was cut off before she had the opportunity to speak.

"Are you guys ready?"

They nodded and made their way toward Keirra's car. She drove toward the vacant field where the bonfire pile was waiting. They filed out of the car waving to old friends, co-workers, and neighbors.

Kayla looked back at them. "Let's get a good spot."

Kristen let Kayla walk ahead and grabbed Keirra by the arm when she went to follow. "I just want to let you know you look beautiful tonight."

Keirra grinned, and Kristen hugged her before they moved closer to the bonfire where the band, drill team, cheerleaders, and flag corps were warming up. Kristen smiled. She could remember the day of the bonfire when they had been in high school. It had been one of the most exciting times in their life or at least it had been in hers.

Seven came and passed, and the bonfire was lit. The band played, and the cheerleaders, flag corps and drill team performed. The school fight song was played, and after a few words from the mayor, principal, and head football coach, the pep rally was dismissed, and most of the crowd headed to the barn where the annual dance was held, others went to the square, and others went home. Kristen and her sisters decided to go to the barn. When they arrived, a good number of people were already there. They found a table close to the floor and had a seat. The music was already blaring and a fast country tune. A few couples began to head to the dance floor.

Kayla sat down next to Kristen. "Is Randy going to be here?"

She nodded. "Yes, he is. He worked late, but he'll be here."

And she couldn't wait because she hadn't seen him at all this week. Due to their hectic schedules, they had missed each other, but they had managed to talk several times. Her thoughts were interrupted when a shadow fell over the table. Looking up, she saw it was Eric. She smiled even though she was a little disappointed because she had been hoping it was Randy.

"Good evening, ladies."

She greeted him in unison with her sisters. Eric's eyebrows rose when Keirra spoke to him. Kristen laughed unable to blame him for his shock.

"Would you like to dance?"

Kristen watched several expressions cross Keirra's face. For a brief moment, she looked like she would take Eric's hand but instead shook her head.

"No, thank you."

Before he could question Keirra, Kristen slid her hand into his and stood up. "Well, I would love to dance."

She winked at him. She liked Eric. He was a good guy. She would give him pointers on how to deal with Keirra. Eric's hand tightened around hers, and he led her to the dance floor. They slid right into a quick two-step with ease.

Eric looked down at her with a grin on his face. "So do you think this will work?"

Keirra sighed. "My sister doesn't want to admit it, but she likes you."

Eric laughed. "Well, she has a funny way of showing it."

She gave him a kind smile. "Just give her time, and don't forget she can't stand competition."

Eric nodded then gave someone over her shoulder a wink. She turned her head to look and saw that he was winking at Keirra. Kristen stifled a laugh when Keirra averted her gaze. She thought it was cute. The music slowed down, and Kristen laughed.

"Now is the time to put on a show."

Before he could ask her what she meant, Kristen stepped closer to him and laughed. "Here she comes in five . . . four . . . three . . . two . . . one."

Eric looked confused, but it quickly disappeared when he looked over her shoulder. A second later, Keirra tapped her on the shoulder.

"Do you mind if I cut in?"

Kristen pretended like she had to think about it then shook her head. She stepped back, and Eric pulled Keirra into his arms. Kristen turned to head toward the table only to stop when someone called her name. She turned in the direction of the voice and waved when she saw Todd standing there. They had been in a few the same classes back in high school. He still looked the same, just a little taller. She smiled at him when he approached her.

"Hi, Todd. How have you been?"

He gave her a quick hug. "Good and yourself?"

"I'm good. Are you having a good time tonight?"

He chuckled. "I am, but it would be a lot better if you would dance with me."

She looked around for Randy but didn't see him. This was a song she liked, and she did come to dance. One dance with Todd wouldn't hurt. Looking back at Todd, she gave him a small nod.

"Sure, I would like to dance with you."

She stepped into Todd's embrace and allowed him to lead her around the dance floor. After a few spins, the song ended, and another began. She looked up at Todd and smiled.

"Have you been in Baxley all this time?"

He nodded. "After graduation, I went to work with my dad. I enjoy what I do. What about you?"

"Well, you know my sisters and I left for college, but we always intended to come back to Baxley. This always felt like home more than anywhere else."

Todd shrugged. "I have to be honest. I didn't think that you and your sisters would come back when you left. Most people who leave don't."

She laughed. "So I have noticed."

Todd's smile slipped a little. "Once you and Randy broke up, I didn't think you would."

Kristen sighed softly. "Sometimes plans change, but you just make new ones."

Todd leaned closer. "Have you made new ones?"

She looked up at Todd with confusion. "What do you mean?"

Todd was quiet for a few steps around the dance floor. "Are you seeing anyone?"

Her mouth dropped open in shock. "Uh . . . well, Randy and I have started seeing each other again."

Todd gave her an inquisitive look. "Is it serious?"

She paused. "To be honest with you, Todd, I'm not sure. Randy and I have a few things to work out."

Todd sighed. "I understand. You and Randy have a lot of history."

She gave Todd a kind look. "You and I have history as well. Just not that kind of history."

Todd gave her a disappointed look. "I know, but it didn't hurt to try."

The song came to an end, and she grinned. "You're right, Todd. It doesn't."

She placed a kiss on his cheek. "Thank you for the dance. Save another for me later if the other women here aren't hanging off of you."

Todd laughed and touched the brim of his hat. "I will."

Kristen turned and headed toward the table. Todd had given her a lot to think about. The main thing being why his touch didn't leave her unable to think like Randy's did. She sat down at the table she and her sisters picked out, but both of them were on the dance floor. Keirra was still dancing with Eric, and Kayla was dancing with Jonah. She wondered what was up between the two of them. Jonah was a good guy, and he was friends with Randy. She scanned the room to see if she could find him, but she couldn't. A sigh of disappointment fell from her lips. She didn't realize how much she wanted to see Randy until now. She wanted things to work out with him, but she couldn't figure out how.

"Hey, beautiful."

Kristen looked up at the sound of Randy's voice. She had begun to count down the time to when he was going to show up.

She smiled. "Hey, you."

"Did you miss me?"

She laughed. "Of course I did."

He held his hand out to her. "Would you like to dance?"

She nodded. "Yes, I would." She paused. "Where is Wade?"

"Mom and Dad insisted he stay with them. They are down at the square."

She was glad his parents helped him like they did. It was tough being a single parent, and she gave Randy all the credit in the world for doing it the way he did. She allowed him to pull her into a standing position before leading the way to the dance floor. When they reached the dance floor, Randy pulled her into his arms and gave her a brief but passionate kiss. When he lifted his head, she was breathless.

"What was that for?"

He smiled. "Because I missed you."

He continued to lead them around the floor. "Did your grandparents make it off all right?"

She laid her head on his shoulder. "Yes, they did, and after my conversation with them, they are thinking about trading in the RV for a home here in Baxley. However, they did try to add in the stipulation of great-grandchildren with the deal."

He laughed. "I have always liked your grandparents, and I think it would be good for all of you for them to move here, great-grandchildren or not."

"I know. I am just glad they were willing to listen to me."

He gave her a puzzled look. "Did you think they wouldn't?"

She shook her head. "Sometimes I think my grandparents keep busy so they aren't always reminded of everything they've lost."

Randy nodded, and she knew it made sense to him because he knew her family history well. Her grandparents only had one child because her grandmother had suffered complications while in childbirth, and an emergency hysterectomy had been performed. Kristen couldn't imagine how difficult that would be on anyone. In the short time she had spent with Wade, he had become special to her, and if something happened to him, she would be crushed, not to mention Randy. She was just glad everything was working out okay with Kristen and her sisters. They had been devastated when they had first come to Baxley. The loss of their father had been fresh, and there had been a lot of grief. Still, they had managed to make it through by supporting each other.

Randy smiled at Kristen. "Did I tell you look beautiful tonight?"

She grinned. "Yes, you did."

"Well then let me tell you again. You look beautiful."

She brushed a speck off of his shoulder. "You look quite handsome yourself."

He was dressed in a green polo shirt that emphasized his broad shoulders and strong arms. Khaki pants covered his bottom half showing off muscular thighs and a firm butt. The man was sexy as sin. She could remember being the envy of a lot of girls.

Dating an older guy who just happened to be sexy and very popular helped fuel the envy. Her arms tightened around him reflexively.

"Let's go somewhere private."

She looked up at with surprise. "Okay."

He took her hand and led her off the dance floor. She spoke to people as they passed by. Randy led her outside to his truck, and she climbed in on the passenger side. She watched Randy walk around to the driver side. When he got in beside her she smiled. "This wasn't an excuse to get me into the backseat was it?"

He chuckled. "As tempting as that sounds no it isn't."

He was silent, and after a long pause, she scooted closer to him. "So why did you bring me out here?"

Randy turned to look at her with an expression she couldn't decipher. "To talk."

She gave him a questioning look. "About?"

He looked away from her and his hands tightened on the steering wheel. He swallowed a few times before looking back at her. "Us."

She exhaled softly. "Okay."

Randy gave her a grim smile. "I saw you dancing with Todd tonight."

Her eyes narrowed at his expression. She was here to have a good time tonight. The last thing she wanted was to have a heated argument with him. Not here. Not now. "And?"

He looked away from her again to stare out the window. His body language told her this was hard for him to talk about. After a few heartbeats of silence he sighed. "I was jealous."

Her eyebrows rose. This was the last thing she expected him to admit. "Why were you jealous?"

Randy frowned. "Because I didn't like seeing another mans hands on you. Anymore than you would like seeing another woman's hands on me."

"Yes, but I trust you."

He sighed. "I trust you as well. In more ways than you know. Otherwise, I wouldn't have told you everything that I have about what happened between Lila and myself. You know things that other people don't."

Shock traveled through her. "I do?"

He nodded. "You do. I care about you more than I think I can ever get you to understand, Kristen, but we can't continue like this. It isn't fair to either of us to only get fifty percent when we both deserve a hundred."

He sighed with aggravation. "This is driving me insane. I'm trying to be patient, Kristen, but I needed to know if we are going to be together all the way or not."

He reached across the truck and took her hand in his. "I just need to know that you want a relationship with me as much as I want one with you. I need to know that you are going to fight for me the way I'm fighting for you."

Kristen closed her eyes. Randy was saying everything that she wanted to hear, and he was backing it up with his action. When she thought about it, he was right. He had been giving her everything that he had, but she wasn't doing the same in return. She was dragging her feet with him, and she couldn't remember why. Yes, Randy broke up with her for a stupid reason, but they had been young. She could have handled things differently than she did. She could have fought for Randy, but she hadn't. Her eyes popped open. *Why didn't I fight for Randy*? Kristen groaned. All this time she wanted to place the blame for the fallout of their relationship on Randy, but she could have done things differently as well. It wasn't fair for her to continue to hold him accountable when she was just as guilty. As the realization struck her, she shook her head. Well she did want Randy, and she always had. This time she was willing to fight for him.

She glanced over at him. His intense gaze was on her. She sighed. "You are right, Randy. It isn't fair to either of us to only go at this halfheartedly. I also realized something else tonight when I was dancing with Todd." She gave his hand a light squeeze. "Your touch is the only one that I want, the touch I crave, the touch I need."

A slow smile spread across his face, and he leaned closer to her. "Does this mean we are going steady?"

She laughed. "I don't think they have called it that since the sixties, but yes we are going steady."

"Good. I promise you won't regret it."

His lips came down on hers, and she opened her mouth to him. A short time later, he pulled back.

"I promise you will never regret this. Now let's get back inside because I love the feel of you in my arms, and I plan to have you in them all night."

She didn't have time to respond before he backed away and climbed out of the truck. Her thoughts were racing as he led her back inside. Randy was true to his word because he tugged her onto the dance floor. A slow song was on, and he gathered her close. She rested her head on his shoulder and enjoyed his embrace. Unfortunately, it didn't last long because the slow song went off and a fast song came on. The floor cleared some, but most people stayed on the floor. Randy leaned back and looked at her with a wicked grin.

"Do you remember our old moves?"

Kristen nodded. There was no way in the world she could forget dancing with Randy. It had been something they had in common and something they had done a lot of. They had even won a few dance contests together. Before she could say anything, Randy spun her out and drew her back in. She emitted a breathless laugh.

"I just had to test you to make sure."

He spun her out again, and they continued around the dance floor. After a few times around the dance floor, she realized most of the attention was on her and Randy.

The song was about to end and she took a deep breath right as Randy took her into a continuous spin. After all the times they danced together she knew what to do. When the song ended, he brought her into him and stopped. There was a lot of applause, but the music resumed, and everyone began dancing again. She had missed this. Until this exact moment she hadn't realized just how much. Being back here with Randy made her happy.

She leaned back and looked at him a little winded. "I don't know about you, but I need a break."

He nodded and led the way off of the dance floor. Keirra and Eric were sitting at their table. Kristen felt her eyes widen when she saw her sister laugh at something Eric said. She had never seen Keirra amused by anything Eric said. To mention Eric's name was enough to make her sister frown. She walked up to the table, and then took a seat next to Keirra.

Keirra smiled at her. "The two of you looked good out there."

She grinned. "To be honest, I am surprised I remembered all of the old moves."

Randy sat down next to her taking a deep breath. "It was like we never stopped dancing."

Kristen laughed. "I know."

He stood. "I am going to go and get some punch. Would you ladies like any?"

They all said yes, so Eric stood up to go with him. Once the two men were out of ear shot Kristen turned to look a Keirra. "So what is going on between you two?"

Keirra shook her head. "Nothing. Just being nice."

Kristen's eyebrows rose. "Oh, is that all?"

Keirra laughed. "What can I say?"

Kristen leaned forward to whisper. "You can say Eric is the finest man you have ever seen, and you are interested in him."

Keirra reached out and took her sister's hand in hers. There was sincerity in her gaze when she spoke. "How about it is Friday night, and I am here to have a good time, and Eric just so happens to be the person I'm having fun with."

Kristen sat back and smiled. "Okay, I can go for that tonight."

Her sister had come a long way, and she didn't want to ruin any of the progress. Having Keirra in the same room with Eric for more than five minutes without an argument ensuing was close to a miracle. She didn't care because Keirra was happy. Come to think of it, so was she.

Chapter Thirteen

Kristen smiled while she watched Randy work on Wade's bike. They were in the backyard, and Randy had been on his knees for fifteen minutes trying to repair the bike Wade had wrecked with daredevils antics. She wasn't going to pretend she hadn't almost had a massive coronary when Wade jumped the curb, especially when he teetered to the side. Before he right himself, she had been certain she was going to have to make an unplanned trip to the emergency room. It seemed Wade had done this several times before. She was tempted to let the bike remain in the state it was in but Wade loved the bike. Now she was glad Randy had strapped the bike helmet, knees and elbow pads on Wade. After what she had seen him do earlier he might need more padding. She couldn't recall her or her sister's being so adventurous. Well okay maybe Keirra had been because of her tomboy streak, but her sister had never pulled any daredevil antics on her bike. She and Wade handed him every tool he called out.

"Wade, this is why you shouldn't jump curbs."

Kristen laughed "You have a Tony Hawk on your hands."

Randy looked up at her and laughed himself. "Not really since I believe Tony Hawk is a skater."

Kristen shrugged her indifference. She had come over to spend time with him and Wade. She smiled at the sight they made. Randy was doing his best to repair the bike with Wade watching his every move. Randy put the wrench down, and she handed him a towel so he could wipe his hands.

"Don't tire yourself out."

He chuckled. "Fixing a bike isn't going to tire me out. He pulled her into his arms. "Why would you be concerned that it would?"

She stretched up to whisper in his ear. "Well I thought we should take advantage having the house to ourselves tonight after we drop Wade off at your moms."

She pulled back and chuckled at his wicked smile. "And what do you think we should do to take advantage of that time?"

The suggestions Randy whispered in her ear had her wanting to gather Wade up and take him over to Ophelia's immediately. He released her from his embrace.

"Now if you want me to make good on any of those promises, I need to make sure this bike is fixed. Wade will want to take it with him."

She nodded and stepped back watching him as he knelt before the bike again. Her heart swelled with happiness. She was back where she wanted to be and she was content. No, she was more than content, she was ecstatic and she was ready to build a stronger relationship with Randy.

He checked the chain on the bike, inspecting his handy work. He must have found something else wrong because he picked up the wrench again. He began tightening a bolt by the wheel and the house phone rang. "Could you answer that for me?"

She nodded and headed into the house. She picked up the ringing phone and spoke. There was a brief pause before a woman's voice came over the line.

"Um . . . I was looking for Randy."

Kristen put the woman on hold and walked toward the patio door leading to the backyard with the cordless extension. Randy was bent over the bike again with the wrench in his hand.

"It's for you."

"Who is it?"

She shrugged. "I didn't ask."

He gave her a strange look before putting down the wrench. Randy cleaned his hands on the towel then reached for the phone before giving her another kiss on the lips. It took her a few moments to get her mind back in focus. The funny thing was it always did when he touched her. There was so much about him she just couldn't get enough of.

Randy had worked hard to convince her to date him even though she cared a lot about him and wanted to be back with him. She had been afraid of what he represented even back then. Randy was a good friend and an even better boyfriend. Those were things in him she knew she would never find in another man. If she had, she didn't remember but it did not matter. The Randy she was dealing with now was more mature more polished. He was hers.

Wade interrupted her mental rambling by asking for some water so she led him toward the house. He slipped his hand inside of hers and held it while they entered the kitchen. She gave him some water in his water bottle and a graham cracker to give him energy he didn't need. She put him at the table before going back to the patio door. Randy liked graham crackers, too, and she wanted to know if he wanted her to bring him a few. When she stepped out the door she knew something was wrong. Randy looked tense and angry. Also every other word that came out of his mouth was a cuss word.

"For the last time I said *no!*"

He hung up the phone, and she could tell he wanted to throw it, but he controlled himself. Although his tight grip on the phone wasn't any better. Kristen had to keep her mouth from dragging the ground. She had never seen Randy lose his temper. Ever.

"Who was it?"

He turned to face her and looked a little surprised to find her standing behind him.

"Lila."

Kristen struggled to keep her expression blank. She never expected to hear that name. "What did she want?"

Randy knelt back down beside the back and sighed with irritation. "She wants to see Wade because she misses him and wants to see how he is."

"Why won't you let Lila see him? Didn't you say that you wanted her to be concerned about him?"

He looked at her like she had just asked him to jump in front of a fast moving car. "Wade doesn't need someone like her in his life."

"Don't you think he needs to make that decision?"

"When he's old enough, yes, but until then I have no choice but to say no on his behalf."

He looked at her, and she saw pain in his eyes. "What do I do when she leaves Wade again? Because trust me she will. It's who she is." He gave her a sad smile. "But don't worry about it. This is my problem."

She frowned. "Don't you mean our problem? I am your girlfriend."

"But not my wife. Being his father makes me the one responsible for his well-being."

Kristen felt reeled back like she had been slapped in the face. She was speechless to the point that her knees trembled.

How could he be so cold? Not to mention that once again he had made a decision about their relationship without her input. It made her wonder if he even had any intention of making her his wife or even including her in his life. She tried to compose herself when she felt more like screaming, but it was difficult. It took all of the years of training she had to keep from hitting Randy in the face. It wasn't often she felt like resorting to violence. She needed to get away from him and quick.

She nodded slowly. "You're right. I'm not your *wife,* and right now, I don't want to be your *girlfriend* either."

Wade came back into the room oblivious to their argument, and she was glad because she didn't want to expose him to it. She turned and opened up the patio door, and Wade ran out. He ran straight for his bike his father had managed to fix. Tears came to her eyes, but she held them back.

"I will be going now. Tell Wade good-bye for me."

Her hands were shaking when she gathered up her purse. She walked out the front door and headed to her car. Her chest ached from the anger she felt. Hurt. Disappointment. Just when she decided to open herself up to him again. Made the choice to put it all on the line. Now he had hurt her again and with the ultimate words. No she hadn't expected Randy to propose marriage tomorrow but she was hoping it would become a reality someday. After the words he just said to her he wondered if the thought had even crossed his mind. The words he said to her in the car a week ago at the dance seemed so heartfelt. Now she couldn't help but to doubt them. How could a man run so hot one second and cold the next? How could he imply that she didn't have Wade's best interest at heart? She cared about Wade just as much as she cared about Randy. She would never do anything to harm either of them. To hear Randy doubt her feelings hurt, a lot. It wasn't until she made it to the house that tears began to fall.

Kayla and Keirra rushed forward in concern and embraced her. "What happened?"

Kristen shook her head. "I don't want to talk about it right now."

It was all she could do to force the words past her tight throat. Her sisters remained silent when they led her to the couch. Keirra's arm automatically went around Kristen. Kayla went in searched of a box of Kleenex. They all sat there while Kristen cried on and off. She managed to pull herself together and was ready to talk. Keirra and Kayla were appalled by the time she finished. Kayla stood up. "This calls for a half gallon of Banana Walnut."

She left and went into the kitchen and returned a short while later with the ice cream and three spoons. Kristen blew her nose and set the tissue aside.

"What could make him say something like that to me? I haven't done anything to deserve this."

Keirra shook her head. "He's angry."

Kayla opened the ice cream, and from the dent left in the rim, it was obvious she was angry. "But it doesn't give him the right to treat Kristen like crap. He has already put her through enough as it is. She gave him another chance in spite of it, and this is how he repays her."

Keirra scoffed. "We have all said things in the heat of moment we didn't mean. I know I have."

Kristen sniffled, looking back and forth between her sisters. If she didn't know any better she would have sworn they switched places judging by their reactions. She sniffled again, while she scooped up a spoonful of the ice cream and ate it. "You could be right. We just need some time apart. He needs to clear his head, and I need to clear mine. We rushed into this too fast."

Kayla gave her a look of utter shock. "Kristen, this has nothing to do with rushing anything. This is pure stupidity."

Keirra nodded. "Kayla would know."

The comment earned her a dirty look from Kayla, and Kristen laughed even though she didn't want to. She knew her sister's were just doing their best to make her feel better. What she would like to do is punch something, hard. Instead, she ate another spoonful of the ice cream. "After this I'm going to take a hot bath and go to bed."

When neither of her sisters protested, she stood and made her way upstairs. In the blink of an eye, the day had gone from good to bad. Now all she wanted to do was hide out in her room until she could figure this all out. She would find a way to get through this.

* * * *

Randy knew the moment Kristen left he made a mistake. He picked up the wrench and threw it to the ground. It stuck in the soft dirt, but it did nothing to expel the anger he felt. Lila had no right to call and ask to see Wade. She had given up her rights a long time ago. He knew he was right in his decision to not let Lila see Wade, but he felt he was dead wrong in how he had explained it to Kristen. To be honest, there hadn't been much discussion of the whole story with Kristen so how could he blame her for her line of questions? He felt sick at the recollection of the expression on Kristen's face. The last time he had seen it was when he told her the reason why he called off their relationship. The look of hurt had been one he had never wanted to see again but yet he managed to put the same exact expression there again. Wade rushed by him toward the house. A second later, he came back out onto the patio with a confused expression on his face.

"Where's Kristen?"

Randy stumbled to find something to say to Wade to explain the difficult situation. He had always been honest with his son, and he wasn't going to change that now. He knelt down to Wade's level.

"Kristen and I had an argument, but I need to go talk to her."

Wade still looked confused. "Are you going to bring her back?"

Randy felt a pain shoot through his heart. There was no way that he could leave things the way they were. He and his son needed Kristen in their lives.

"I will do my best. Now, go inside and pack a few toys. We are going to Grandma's house."

Wade nodded, and Randy reached for his cell phone and dialed his parents' number. His mother answered quickly.

"Mom, I need you to watch Wade for me. I will explain later."

His mother paused before agreeing to watch Wade. A short while later, he was driving toward his parents' home. His mother stood on the porch waiting for them, and he gave her an apologetic look as he walked up.

"Thanks, Mom. I know this is last minute."

Her look was full of curiosity, but she didn't ask. "Which tells me whatever it is must be important."

He sighed. "It is, Mom. I messed up big time with Kristen. I don't know if I can fix things, but I have to try. I didn't know what had been missing from my life until Kristen came back into it. I made the mistake of not fighting for her the first time. I won't make that mistake again. If it is late I won't wake you."

She embraced him. "If you need to leave Wade here overnight you can."

He kissed his mother on the cheek, always grateful for her. She was there whenever he needed her, and he appreciated it. He turned and left contemplating what he was going to say to Kristen. He would speak from his heart and hope she was willing to listen.

The drive to her house seemed to take longer than it had before, but he finally arrived. He cut the engine and took a deep breath to calm his nerves before opening the truck door and stepping out. He walked up the driveway to the walkway and stopped in front of the door. Taking a deep breath, he knocked on the door. A few seconds later the door was opened and a glowering Keirra stood behind it.

"I was wondering if you would show up."

Randy held his hands up as a peace offering. Keirra stepped back and let him in. He took a step inside and was confronted by Kayla. To make her mad was to get into serious trouble. Her tongue could be sharper than Keirra's when it needed to be.

"This is what happens when they come in threes," he muttered under his breath to himself.

"Look, I know you are Kristen's sisters, and you care about her a lot, but this is something we have to work out."

Keirra shocked him. "I agree. For some reason, my sister cares about you no matter how many times you hurt her. However, you better make it right. If you don't, I will let Kayla tear into you, and whatever she doesn't get, I will finish off."

Kayla sputtered as Keirra pulled her from the room. If Randy didn't have the ability to tell them apart, he would have sworn they had switched places. He turned and headed up the stairs before realizing he had no idea which room was hers. Walking to the second door on the left, he decided to try it first because it was her old bedroom from what he remembered. He knocked and heard Kristen call out for him to enter. Opening the door he stepped inside and closed the door behind him. She looked up in surprise cleaning her nose with a Kleenex. Beautiful didn't begin to describe the way she looked. Even with swollen eyes, blotched cheeks, and a red nose. To know he was responsible for it made him feel like the jerk he was.

Kristen glared at him, and he paused. She had never looked at him with hostility. Not even when he signed Wade up for her day care center. He knew he was in deep, and it was going to take some serious work on his end to get out of it.

"What are you doing here?"

He walked over to the bed and had a seat. "I came to talk to you."

Kristen put the stuffed bear she held aside. "Well, I can't believe my sisters let you in."

He gave her a kind smile. "I got lucky."

The look she gave him was indescribable. There had never been a time when he hadn't been able to tell what she was thinking, but this time, he couldn't decipher what those brown eyes were saying to him. Right now, they were a blank slate.

"What if I told you I don't want to talk?"

He sighed in frustration. "I would believe you, but I would still try to plead my case."

She crossed her arms over her chest, and he knew he was in for a tough apology, but he went for it anyway. "I made a mistake, and I came back to correct it."

Her expression grew even more shuttered. "It seems you have a habit of making mistakes. It's too late."

He smiled at her well-placed jab at him. "No, I don't think it's too late for us. If it was, you wouldn't still be wearing the locket nor would you be holding the teddy bear I gave you." He took the bear from her. "I can't believe you still have this."

"I can't believe I have it either," she muttered.

He ignored her and studied the bear. It was in pretty good condition considering its age, which told him she had taken good care of it. Like he planned to take good care of her for the rest of his life if she would let him. Randy handed the stuffed animal back to her. "I'm sorry for the mean things I said earlier. I was angry and let myself get out of control."

Truth was she was a part of his life and was going to become a bigger part of his life if he had anything to do with it. It meant he would share his problems with her, and she would share her problems with him.

"Will you forgive me?"

She kept her expression neutral, and he realized this was going to be more difficult than he thought. "No, for the pain you have put me through, I would still like to hear you grovel a little. This is the second time you have made a decision with something concerning our relationship without consulting me. It's irritating." She paused. "No, it pisses me off. If we are going to move forward in this *relationship,* I need to know if I am I an *equal partner*."

"You are," he replied without hesitation. "I'm just not good at showing it."

She sighed, and he knew she wasn't convinced, but she was giving it consideration. "No, Randy. You aren't good at showing it. What is it you want from me because I'm trying to figure it out, and I don't know."

Randy slid off the bed and got on his knees. "Be patient with me. Kristen, I don't have all the answers, but I swear I'm trying."

He closed his eyes. "I'm going to make mistakes along the way, but I can't live without you in my life. I know because I have tried to before, and it sucked. I can't give up on us, Kristen, because of what we have had."

He gave her a pleading look. "We can have that again. It might not be the same exact relationship, but I don't want it to be. I want us to build on that. Just like we have evolved into different people our relationship should as well."

He watched as tears welled in Kristen's eyes, and he closed his eyes. "Please, Kristen. I'm not going anywhere this time. I won't give up like I did six years ago."

He opened his eyes when she didn't respond. There was an indescribable expression on her face. When she spoke her voice was soft but full of emotion. "It isn't going to be easy, Randy. You aren't the only one who can make decisions about us. I'm not saying I have a final say so in what goes on with Wade, but at least discuss it with me." She paused. "He is a part of *our* relationship, and decisions concerning him affect us."

He took her hands in his. "I know, and I'm sorry. You have my word. I will never do it again. I know Wade means a lot to you, and I respect you for accepting and treating him like he is yours. I know it's been difficult for you."

She gave him a look of surprise, and he smiled. "No, I didn't read your thoughts. I read mine. I have thought about it a lot, and I would love for Wade to be ours. He already is in the ways that matter."

Tears began flowing down Kristen's cheeks, and he knew it was for a different reason this time. He wanted Kristen to be Wade's mother, and with Lila having given up her parental rights, he was more than willing to make it official. He couldn't think of anyone he would rather have as the mother of his children than Kristen.

She sniffled and gave him a watery smile. "That means a lot to me, Randy."

His hands tightened on hers. "And you mean the world to me."

She gave a slight nod. "And you to me."

He stared at her before leaning closer to her giving her a sexy grin. "So I can say we are back together?"

She shook her head at his expression and laughed. "I just realized I'm not sure we were ever apart, but yes, you can say we are. Why?"

"I have to have good news to report to Wade. He told me I had to get you back, and I promised I would."

Kristen smiled. "Well, you can tell Wade you were successful in getting me back."

He reached over and pulled her into his arms, and she looked up at him. "So where do we go from here?"

Her smile widened, and he realized just how much he'd missed it. "I was hoping to continue to work on our relationship, but this time I want to get it right."

She gave him a puzzled look. "What do you mean?"

He brought her hands up to his lips and kissed them. "I want a future with you. I want you to be my wife, and I want to add to our family."

Her eyebrows rose. "Do you have a timeline to get this done?"

He nodded. "It will happen when we are ready for it to happen, but I just wanted to let you know what my intentions were. I don't want to make the same mistake I did the last time."

She laughed. "That sounds good to me."

Randy didn't pick up Wade until the next morning, but when he did, Wade was awaiting the news. His son couldn't contain himself when he heard Kristen was back, and Randy let Wade bounce around uncontained. He couldn't blame his son because his own excitement threatened to spill over. Just like Wade, he was looking forward to spending his future with Kristen, and it was beginning now.

About the Author

Stephanie Morris resides in Fort Worth, Texas. She has no children of her own, but has three nieces and one nephew and is proud to call Rocky, her three-year-old dog, her child. In her spare time, she enjoys reading, traveling, dancing, cooking, and spending time with her friends and family. She has been writing for several years now and has written several works in erotica and romance. This is her first published work, and she is looking forward to several more. She can be reached on MySpace at www.myspace.com/stephaniemorrisbooks or at www.stephaniemorris.webs.com.

Amira Press, LLC
www.amirapress.com

Activity Partner
by Nitanni Chionne

Cassie James is an African American single mom who has just about given up on the idea of love. Dr. Ethan Quinn is of English descent, a widower who recently moved from Boston to Chicago with his daughter. Both meet at a tee ball practice, and realize they have a couple of things in common—they're single parents and their social lives are on life support.

Hitting it off, the two decide to become activity partners—attending each other's events and helping each other out with babysitting when need be. The two become more than friends, and their past begins to haunt them both. Cassie is faced with the prospect of trusting and loving again. Ethan knows about love, and wants to love her, but also has to face the fear of having and losing love.

Made in the USA